Mills & Boon
Best Seller Romance

A chance to read and collect some of the best-loved novels from Mills & Boon—the world's largest publisher of romantic fiction.

Every month, six titles by favourite Mills & Boon authors will be re-published in the *Best Seller Romance* series.

A list of other titles in the *Best Seller Romance* series can be found at the end of this book.

Rachel Lindsay

CHATEAU IN PROVENCE

MILLS & BOON LIMITED
LONDON · TORONTO

First published 1973
Australian copyright 1982
Philippine copyright 1982
This edition 1982

© Scribe Associates 1973

ISBN 0 263 73992 9

Set in 9 on 12 pt Plantin

02-0982

Made and printed in Great Britain by
Richard Clay (The Chaucer Press) Ltd,
Bungay, Suffolk

CHAPTER ONE

ALAIN MAURY was in a foul temper. It was apparent in the set of his wide slim shoulders, in the tightness of his mouth and the narrowing of his eyes, their warm brown darkened by his thoughts. He had placed his final hopes on the Cromerty Institute in California, and since *they* could not help him discover why the blue rose had no scent, he must abandon the project.

Yet how could he bring himself to do so? This rose was his last chance to prove he had not lost his creative talent. Ever since he had propagated it in his laboratory in Grasse its magic fragrance had haunted him, firing him with the determination to make a new perfume. But incredibly the blue rose – when grown under normal conditions in earth – had no scent whatever, and the only other choice – to grow it in special greenhouses – was far too expensive to be practical.

He sighed. It was four years since he had produced Eternelle, and he was haunted by the fear that he might never again be able to create anything that would capture the market in the same way. What a success it had been – still was for that matter – doing for Adrienne Cosmetics what Number 5 had done for Chanel.

He flung the letter from the Institute on to his desk. At thirty he was too young to live on the success of his past; unless he could create more new scents he would return to the pharmaceutical side of the business.

He stared through the windows at the beautifully landscaped grounds that extended for several thousand hectares round the house, a tangible sign – as was the enormous white building in Grasse where his mother's perfumes were made –

of her great success. A success he had done nothing to increase since Lucille's death.

Lucille . . . He clenched his hands. When would her memory cease to torment him?

Light steps crossed the floor and he swung round, forcing a smile as his mother came in. From a distance she looked as young as her silver-framed photograph on his desk, though as she came closer he saw the fine lines around her eyes and the speckle of grey in the glossy black hair that curved into a classical coil on the nape of her neck.

Strange, he mused, that a woman who had built her fortune on artifice should use so little herself. Today, he would swear, she wore only a touch of lipstick and her special scent – the first one he had ever made.

"Why the frown?" she asked, her soft voice troubled.

In curt tones he told her of the letter from the Cromerty Institute.

"Forget the blue rose and concentrate on something else," she said when he had finished.

"I can't forget it." His voice, though light in timbre, had an edge to it, giving indication of the quicksilver temperament he tried – not always with success – to keep under control. "Do you know how long it's been since I've produced anything worthwhile?"

"You're not idle. You look after the financial side of the business. Why worry about scent? Anyway, we don't need another one. You want it for *your* satisfaction."

"I'm well aware of that!" he cried. "Lucille's been dead for three years, and since then I've created nothing. Nothing!"

"Give yourself time."

Adrienne Maury sank down on a velvet settee. In everything she did she was elegant, and looking at her serene face it was hard to believe that – left a widow with a five-year-old boy – she had had sufficient tenacity to make her own beauty prod-

6

ucts and sell them from door to door until her fame had spread to the point where a local bank had agreed to finance her, setting her on the first step to international success.

She spoke little of the early, back-breaking years, though Alain could remember returning from school and having nowhere to do his homework, so crowded had their tiny flat been with bowls of lotions in varying stages of completion.

If only he had his mother's perseverance and control, he thought moodily, instead of a fiery Latin streak that exploded when he least wanted it to. The way it had done the last time he had seen Lucille alive. Lucille . . .

"Come back, Alain," his mother said. "You're miles away."

"I was thinking."

"You think too much. It's time you fell in love again and settled down."

"Is that an order or a request?"

"A hope!"

He smiled, and his face changed as if by magic, showing him to be an unusually good-looking man with the fine-cut features often found in the Latin. There was a mixture of delicacy and strength in his figure: wide-shouldered yet slim-hipped; only average in height but so well co-ordinated he gave the impression of being much taller. His hands were narrow and well-shaped, their restless movement giving the lie to the sardonic coolness with which he generally surveyed the world.

His mother watched him with compassion. It had been given to few women to appreciate this complex son of hers: so easy to love if you understood him; so impossibly difficult if you didn't. And Lucille never had. Not that she could say so to Alain: on the subject of his dead fiancée he brooked no discussion.

"I'm serious about your getting married," she repeated. "Aren't you tired of playing around?"

"No man admits to being tired of that!" He walked to the

7

door. "I'm going for a stroll. If Colette telephones, say I'll call her back."

"Colette," his mother said with such feeling that he laughed.

"You've just been telling me to settle down!"

"Not with her! She's so domineering."

"Perhaps I need someone like that."

He left the room and, crossing the hall, went to stand on the front steps. The trees were still bare, yet already there was a suggestion of birth in the air, of buds waiting to appear and leaves ready to unfurl.

He descended the steps and strode along the drive to the greenhouse. Entering it, he made for a distant corner and a flowering rose bush in a terracotta pot.

His beloved blue rose.

Exquisitely beautiful, it unfurled itself in front of him like a graceful woman disclosing her body. The pale blue petals parted to show a tightly closed heart of deeper blue. A heart without scent, like a woman without a soul.

For a long while he stared at it, his expression growing darker until, with an angry exclamation, he picked up the pot and dashed it to the ground.

The violent gesture exhausted his anger, leaving him calmer than he had been since he had opened the letter from the Cromerty Institute. With calmness came regret for his action, and he bent and picked up the bush. The full-blown roses had broken off and lay on the ground, but several closed buds were still intact and he touched his hand to them and wished he could appreciate beauty for its own sake and not be filled with regret because he could not make the blooms produce a scent.

Unaware that he was still holding the bush in his arms, he left the conservatory and walked through the garden. The cultivated lawns were soon left behind and the landscape grew wilder. Deep in thought, he walked unseeingly, and only the darkening of the day made him realise he had come round the side of the far mountain and was standing on Chambray land.

It was hard to believe that, as the crow flies, he had barely come a couple of miles, so different was the terrain here from his own property. It was as though it had never known the hand of man. As indeed it had not, Alain mused, surveying the craggy mountainside where stunted trees clung to sharp inclines and rough boulders marked the precipitous descent to the valley far below.

Even on the brightest day shadows always lay on these slopes, and now, at dusk, the whole area was filled with Stygian gloom, while a coldness seeped up from the icy waters of the mountain stream that rushed headlong through the gorge.

Shivering in his fine cashmere sweater, he turned to retrace his steps. Moving quickly, he stumbled and dropped the rose bush. Once more it lay at his feet, and this time he decided to leave it there. Better to do as his mother had advised and forget it ever existed.

With a sigh he walked on, but after a few steps he halted. He couldn't leave the bush to die. Ashamed of his sentimentality, he went back to it and with quick movements scraped a hole in the flinty ground. By the time he had planted the bush his fingers were bleeding, grazed, and wrapping them in his handkerchief, he straightened and walked on. As far as he was concerned, the blue rose no longer existed.

"Are you sure you won't change your mind?" Mr. Joseph asked Miranda Dixon. "If it's a question of money –"

"You've already been more than generous," she interrupted. "But I've been here two years and unless I start on my own – I feel –"

"Time will pass you by and you'll be a failure at twenty-two!" Mr. Joseph concluded.

Unable to deny the truth of the remark, Miranda smiled, though looking round the large room with its bolts of materials, long trestle tables and rows of dummy figures, she knew

9

she was saying goodbye to one of the most satisfying periods of her life.

From the moment she had come to work as a dress designer for Mr. Joseph she had been a success. Within six months her name was known throughout the trade, and within two years she had become chief designer for the company.

But now she wanted to start on her own, and neither the offer of more money or a partnership could dissuade her.

"You won't produce much of a collection with five hundred pounds," Mr. Joseph said. "If you want to set up alone, at least let me help you."

Miranda shook her head. "I want to be free to design what I like."

"No designer's free," Mr. Joseph responded gloomily. "We might ignore Paris, but we can't ignore the buyers from Selfridges, and Harrods!"

"That's *exactly* what I intend doing!"

Looking at the tall slim girl in front of him, her piquant face arrestingly alive, her wide-apart grey eyes sparkling with determination and her honey-coloured hair glinting red in the electric light, he had no doubt about her future. Success and Miranda were made for each other, and she certainly deserved it more than the young designers he had hired and fired before this hard-working and intelligent girl had come his way.

"I hope you'll come to my first collection," Miranda continued, her beaming smile showing perfect teeth that made her look more American than English.

"Nothing will keep me away," Mr. Joseph assured her. "How else will I be able to steal your designs!"

Strap-hanging her way home in the crowded underground train, Miranda did not feel as confident as she had pretended, and wondered if she had been wise to leave Mr. Joseph. Yet two years was a long time to stay with one firm if you were ambitious to make your own way. Besides, fashions for the young should be designed by the young, and that meant taking

10

a chance before she grew stale and jaded.

The train jerked to a stop and there was a rush to the exit. Propelled upwards on a mass of pushing shoulders, she was soon breathing deeply of the cool night air, her spirits reviving as she wended her way up Hampstead High Street to the block of old-fashioned flats where she lived with her father.

"Is that you, Miranda?" Roger Dixon came out of the living-room to greet her. A well-built man with thick grey hair and brilliant blue eyes in a tanned face, he looked more like a sailor than the engineer he was. "I thought we'd go out for dinner," he went on. "It'll save you the bother of cooking."

"You mean it will save *you* the bother!" Since she had first started work they had shared the household chores, and this week it was her father's turn in the kitchen.

"That thought did cross my mind," he admitted, "but there's another reason too."

"Anything important?"

"I'll tell you later."

When he did, the news was something she had not anticipated, and it was brought to her attention by a sheet of deckle-edged paper which her father held out to her.

Unfolded it, she saw spidery handwriting, and did not need to look at the signature to know it would show the word Chambray. Emilie, Comtesse Chambray.

Miranda dropped the letter to the table. "What does Grandmother want?"

"Read it."

She did so. The letter was short and to the point. Written in precise English, it expressed sorrow at not having seen Miranda for many years and hoped this would be remedied by her coming to spend a holiday in Provence.

"What's the point?" Miranda asked. "I haven't seen her since I was six, and *that* was only for an hour!"

"You reminded her of your mother," Roger Dixon said softly, "and it brought back memories she wanted to forget.

11

That's one reason she didn't see you again."

"I still look like my mother," Miranda replied. "So why should she change her mind?"

"Old people frequently change their mind. Be kind, my dear. You're young and you can afford it."

"How can *you* be kind?" she burst out. "She practically accused you of killing Mother!"

"In her eyes I probably did. She was sure that if Louise hadn't married me and come to live in England, her tuberculosis would have been controlled."

"No one could have guaranteed that."

"This climate certainly didn't help her."

"In those days T.B. was usually fatal," Miranda persisted.

"We're getting off the subject," her father said. "Your grandmother wants to see you and I'd like you to go." He took an airmail ticket from his pocket. "This came with the letter."

Colour flared in Miranda's cheeks. "Does she think we can't afford the fare?"

"I imagine it was sent as a gesture of friendship – not charity. Take it, Miranda. Anyway, France is the home of fashion. You might come back with some ideas!"

"I'm sure to find millions in a village in Provence! Honestly, Dad, you'll have to do better than that!"

He shook his head and remained silent, and watching him, she marvelled that no other woman had succeeded in capturing him. Was the memory of her mother still too strong after twenty years, or was he afraid of allowing himself to become vulnerable again?

She sighed. "All right, I'll go."

"Good. I'm sure you won't have any regrets."

They were words Miranda was to remember with irony and bitterness many times in the months to follow.

CHAPTER TWO

IT was a warm April day when Miranda stepped out of the aircraft at Nice airport, and she found it hard to believe that only two hours before she had been battling with the wind to cross the tarmac at Heathrow. Feeling she had stepped into a fairy-tale world, she had to restrain herself from dancing her way to the white terminal building.

At this time of the season the airport was quiet, though as she passed through Immigration the arrival of an internal flight from Paris was announced.

Soon the air was alive with voluble Gallic voices, and she was pleasantly surprised to find her French was good enough for her to understand what was being said. Perhaps having a French mother had given her an ear for the language.

Clutching her passport, she went in search of her two red cases – a generous going-away present from Mr. Joseph – and then followed the porter to the taxi rank.

A solitary yellow cab was parked beneath the sign and she pointed to it urgently. The porter nodded but did not increase his pace, and from the corner of her eye she saw a dark-haired man striding in the same direction as herself. She quickened her pace, and as though guessing her intention the man did the same. With a defiant lift of her head she broke into a run, silken-clad legs barely touching the pavement, honey-gold hair flying. Simultaneously they reached the cab, and simultaneously put their hands on the door: scarlet-tipped fingers almost touching strong, tanned ones.

"So sorry," Miranda smiled sweetly. "Perhaps you'll wait for the next one."

"Perhaps you would wait instead," the man barked.

"I was here first."

"A debatable point, *mademoiselle*. You know I wanted the taxi and you deliberately ran ahead of me."

"*You* ran ahead of *me*." Firmly keeping her hand on the door, she signalled the porter to put her cases in the boot.

"Do not let us argue about it." The man was equally firm. "The taxi is mine." He swung round and gave a sharp command to the porter who, about to put the red cases in the boot, stopped in mid-air.

"You can't deny you saw me running ahead of you," Miranda said in her calmest tone.

"No one could have missed you in that ridiculous get-up!" Brown eyes raked over her full-skirted emerald suit and jaunty hat with its single scarlet feather.

"Just because I run faster than you," she said furiously, "there's no need to be rude!" She swung round and gave the taxi driver her most ravishing smile. "Please tell this *gentleman* that I was here first."

"But of course, *mademoiselle*." The driver scrambled out of the car, took the cases from the porter and dumped them on the seat beside him.

Only then did Miranda turn to her vanquished neighbour. "I'm sure you won't have long to wait for another taxi."

"You British!" he exclaimed, and turning his back on her, walked away.

Fuming, Miranda settled herself in the seat. So much for French gallantry. And so much for a Frenchman's appreciation of fashion! Ridiculous get-up indeed! This green suit had been the most successful design in her last collection.

"Where are you going?" the driver asked.

"Bayronne," Miranda replied. "Near Grasse."

"That's a long way."

"I know," she replied, to reassure him she understood the journey would be expensive, and then lapsed into silence as she watched the passing scene.

Towering apartment buildings and sprawling two-storey

motels marked by gaudy neon signs bordered the sea front. It was a far cry from the luxury atmosphere she had anticipated, and she realised that this stretch of coastline was the Mecca of the package tour.

The car swung sharply left, speeded for several kilometres along a wide motorway and then branched off on to a winding country road, lined on either side with row upon row of greenhouses.

"Flowers," the driver explained. "We send them all over Europe."

"Don't they grow flowers in Bayronne too?" she asked.

"Around Grasse the flowers are used for making perfume." The man swung round for an instant to grin at her. "Mademoiselle is like a flower herself."

Miranda's ruffled feelings were mollified by the compliment, and only then did she realise how irritated she had been by the argument at the airport. Used to being admired by men, she had found the Frenchman's fury surprising. As if it had mattered all that much for him to wait an extra few minutes for another taxi! Not that she couldn't have waited too, she thought, and probably would have done if he had not been so unnecessarily rude. Pushing him from her mind she concentrated on the countryside.

They were climbing continuously, the narrow road winding its way further and further from the coast. The garish brightness of the sparkling sea, dark green palms and shiny pebbles was replaced by the muted greens of hedgerows and fields, the faded rust of ancient tiled roofs and the dusty grey of crumbling stones. Here was the countryside of Cézanne, though the occasional clumps of purple bougainvillea and showering cascades of pink and red roses brought Bonnard to mind.

Village after village swept by, some a mere cluster of houses and some a cobbled square set with a fountain, a church and the inevitable *bar tabac*. And over it all was the mellow wash of spring sunshine and air fragrant with orange blossom.

Just after one o'clock they reached Bayronne, a single street of houses and shops with several cobbled alleys branching from it. The Chambray Chateau stood at the end of a winding lane outside the village, and they swung through a pair of tall, decaying pillars and along a delapidated drive that only became more carefully tended as they neared the house.

Having only her father's vague description of it, Miranda was unprepared for the fairy-tale splendour of the chateau. In such a place must the Sleeping Beauty have lain for a hundred years: might still be lying, she thought fancifully as she took in the crumbling stone façade and the four turrets whose pointed domes were capped by grey tiles. At ground- and first-floor level the windows were masked by faded wooden shutters, but those in the turrets were narrow slits, more fitting for spy-holes.

Before she could appreciate any more the heavy, nail-studded door opened and an elderly woman came hurrying down the steps to take the cases from the driver.

After paying the man, Miranda went to help her, but the woman shook her head and beckoned her to come inside.

Miranda did so and waited by the door, expecting to see her grandmother, but the hall remained empty and she stared at the enormous tapestry that hung on one wall and stretched from the high vaulted ceiling almost to the ground. Ahead of her wide stone stairs swept up to a galleried first floor, while at ground level some half-dozen closed doors gave indication of the size of the interior. What a large home for one old woman to occupy!

"The Comtesse would like to see you as soon as you are ready," the servant said. "If you wish to wash first I will show you to your room . . ."

Anxious to get the meeting over, Miranda shook her head, and the woman led her across the polished tiled floor into the salon.

Expecting the same decay evident in the rest of the chateau, Miranda was surprised by the room. Straight-backed gilt furniture mingled happily with bow-fronted satinwood chests and brocade-covered settees. A profusion of tables was scattered on the Aubusson carpet, several of them holding bowls of flowers whose colours picked out the flowers beneath her feet. Narrow windows, their edges softened by faded damask curtains, afforded a view of a terrace, beyond which could be glimpsed sloping lawns and tall grass rippling in the breeze.

But it was the woman lying on a pink settee in front of an enormous marble fireplace who commanded her attention. Emilie, Comtesse Chambray. Her grandmother in name only, who had commanded her presence here.

"Come closer, child," a reedy voice requested. "My eyesight is not as good as it used to be."

Slowly Miranda moved forward, realising how false her memory had played her as she looked into the lined face. Here was not the majestic, silver-haired matriarch of her imagination, but a diminutive woman with wispy grey hair, a face as lined as old parchment and liquid brown eyes – her most beautiful feature – set above a high-bridged, aristocratic nose. She was as fine-boned as a sparrow, and not even the cashmere shawl round her shoulders could disguise the thinness of her body.

"Come closer still," the Comtesse commanded, and held out her hands.

Miranda was obliged to take them and found their grip surprisingly strong. Dutifully she placed her lips to the lined cheek. "How are you, Grandmother?"

"All the better for seeing you." She motioned to a chair. "Sit down, child."

Miranda did so and found herself being carefully scrutinised.

"I like your suit," her grandmother said unexpectedly. "Your father wrote and told me you design clothes. You must

17

tell me how you became interested in fashion. I have so much to learn about you."

"Why do you want to bother after so many years?" Miranda asked bluntly.

"Is it ever too late to admit one is wrong?"

"Certain things can never be put right."

"You sound bitter."

"I don't mean to be." Miranda stared at the floor and then, as nothing was said, stole a glance at her grandmother. The woman was lying motionless, her face devoid of expression but her eyes filled with tears that overflowed down the furrowed cheeks. Knowing she was the cause of it, Miranda felt a pang of remorse.

"I don't think we should talk about the past," she said hesitantly. "It won't do any good."

"If talking about it can help you to understand why I behaved the way I did –"

"Not yet," Miranda interrupted. "Let's get to know each other first."

"Very well." The Comtesse was in control of herself again. "I am sure you would like to go to your room and change. Simone will show you the way."

The Comtesse rang a handbell and the servant who had shown Miranda in appeared at the door and led her up the curving stone staircase.

As she had supposed, several corridors branched off from the gallery, each one giving access to two or three rooms. There were at least a dozen bedrooms here apart from those to be found in the turrets.

Plenty to explore, she decided, and felt her pulses stir with excitement. There was an atmosphere in an old house like this that could not be found anywhere else. How she would have loved exploring it as a child: would love it now if she gave herself a chance. But she was not going to do so; she was only here for a couple of weeks and had no intention of becoming

18

attached either to the chateau or her grandmother.

But she was hard pressed to maintain her reserve when, entering a corner bedroom overlooking the back of the chateau, she glimpsed the view through the window. Rolling slopes stretched for mile upon mile: green fields, gold fields and fields of rich brown earth with trees marking the landscape throughout. Cypresses, tall and dark green, pointed stately fingers to the sky, while silvery olive trees – their small leaves catching even the faintest gust of wind – seemed to be constantly dancing.

A slight cough from Simone drew Miranda back to the centre of the room. "Will you be able to find your way downstairs, *mademoiselle*?"

"I think so."

Abruptly the woman walked out, leaving Miranda to wonder at her unfriendliness. She was obviously an old retainer and might be jealous in case her mistress's affections were usurped by a newcomer.

With a shrug she unlocked her cases and unpacked, hanging her clothes in the hand-painted wooden armoire and putting her underwear in the pine chest that flanked the stone wall beside her bed. And what a bed it was! Large enough to hold four people, with an overhead canopy of flowered tapestry identical with the hand-woven rugs on the tiled floor.

Not finding a private bathroom, she ventured along the corridor until she came upon a large, old-fashioned one. But the water that gushed from the taps was surprisingly hot, and quickly she washed her face and ran downstairs.

The salon was empty and she crossed the hall and opened the first door she came to. It was a library, dark and shuttered and smelling of dust and leather. Closing it hurriedly, she tried several more doors before finding herself in the dining room.

It was high-ceilinged and rectangular, with a long narrow table at whose head sat the Comtesse. Tall-backed chairs

19

marked twelve places, and though only two were laid, Miranda had the impression that every chair was occupied by a Chambray ancestor, each one watching her with a disdainful stare.

"How young you look," her grandmother exclaimed, motioning her to sit down. "It's the freedom of dress and hair, I suppose. In my youth we had to be so proper we were old before our time!"

Another elderly retainer – were there no young people in the chateau? Miranda wondered – served them with asparagus, thick and paler than any she had seen before, though tasting delicious, as did the fillet of veal with Calvados and cream and the wafer-thin pancakes served with slices of lemon, which concluded the meal.

"I am glad to see you enjoy your food," the Comtesse remarked.

"When other people cook it for me," Miranda admitted.

"Who does the cooking in your home?"

"My father and I share it."

"Most Frenchwomen are taught to cook," the Comtesse said, "even if circumstances will not require them to do so. A woman who does not understand good cuisine will never have a good table, no matter how excellent her chef."

"English people don't set as much store by food as the French."

"More's the pity."

Miranda bit back a retort, determined to say nothing that might provoke a quarrel.

"We will have coffee in the salon," the Comtesse was saying. "If you will give me your arm . . ."

With a strange reluctance Miranda did so, feeling tall and ungainly beside the fragile old lady.

Re-entering the salon, she sensed a change in the atmosphere and looked around her as she settled her grandmother on the settee. Nothing appeared to have been touched, yet the room was different. Even the smell was – Of course, the smell!

20

She gazed enraptured at the bowls of roses which had been placed on the lacquered tables.

"You are admiring the flowers?" the Comtesse enquired.

"I've never seen blue roses before." Miranda tentatively touched a petal. It was the colour of a delphinium, though its perfume was even more amazing than its shade. "These must be very special. Do you grow them yourself?"

"We don't grow them at all. They are mine by accident!" Seeing Miranda's bewilderment, the Comtesse smiled. "I will tell you the story. You may find it interesting. The first rose was planted – though it would be truer to say it was thrown away and *then* planted – by a young chemist who lives with his mother on the other side of the valley. For several years he tried to grow these roses and failed."

"No blooms, you mean?"

"Plenty of blooms, but no scent. Eventually he abandoned the idea of growing them. He took the last of his plants and threw it away – on my land. A few months later Maurice, my handyman, was out looking for a goat that had strayed and found a bush of blue roses. He picked one and brought it to me."

"You must have been astonished!"

"I was. I decided to take as many cuttings from the bush as we could and plant them in the same area. In a matter of weeks we had a carpet of blue flowers. It was unbelievable."

"Are they a special strain?"

"Yes. Alain's a gifted horticulturist as well as a chemist. It's been of great value to him in his work. He creates perfume," her grandmother explained, "and for that you need flowers. Have you heard of Eternelle?"

"Who hasn't?"

"Alain Maury produced that."

"I see." Miranda pointed to the roses. "But tell me the rest of *this* story."

"Well, for several weeks we had rooms filled with these

roses. They have a scent that invades your senses – almost like a drug." The thin voice stopped apologetically. "I'm afraid you will think me fanciful."

"I know what you mean," Miranda said slowly. "I can feel it too. Please go on."

"There's not much more to tell. I got bronchitis and Alain came to see me with a gift from his mother. When he saw the blue roses he couldn't believe his eyes – or should I say his nose! He practically accused me of spraying them artificially!"

"It's incredible." Miranda looked at a bowl of roses again. Even from a distance their scent was overpowering. "His had no smell at all?"

"None. He had tried everything – without success."

"Until he threw one away on your land." Miranda looked at her grandmother mischievously. "What magic power do you possess? After all, you live in a fairy-tale castle!"

"The magic is in the earth, my child – that much Alain has found out. Millions of years ago this region was volcanic. Many of the boulders you still see around are lumps of lava. The soil in this valley is particularly rich with minerals and it seems that these are in exactly the right proportion for the blue rose to grow properly."

"What's this man going to do? Put the same kind of minerals into *his* land?"

"It wouldn't work. According to geologists it could take years before his land has similar properties to mine; and even then there's no guarantee it will be the same. That's one reason I asked you to come here."

The change of subject left Miranda confused.

"Alain wants to buy my land," the Comtesse explained. "I only need to keep a few hectares around the chateau, and he's offered me an excellent price for the rest. But I wanted to talk to you before I made a decision." The Comtesse shifted on her pillow. "You and my great-nephew Pierre are my only remaining relatives. When I die the chateau and land will be divided between you both."

"My home's in England," Miranda said quickly.

"I know. That is another reason I should not have waited so long before having you here." The thin voice stopped and the silence was heavy with memories. Then the voice resumed, lighter in tone, as if the past had been staved off. "If I accepted Alain's offer I would have considerably more money to leave."

"Or to spend," Miranda said quickly. "The money is yours."

"I am too old to make use of it. Good food is my only extravagance, and even then I can only eat a little. No, Miranda, the important question is whether we keep the property intact – in case you or Pierre wish to make it your home – or whether we sell Alain what he wants. He has offered to buy the house too, if that will help me to make up my mind. He would allow me to live in it until I died, of course."

"How ghoulish!"

"It is practical. You should appreciate the difference."

"You must do as you wish," Miranda murmured. "But I certainly don't want you to leave me anything."

"I am not English enough to leave my money to a cat's home!"

"Leave it to your great-great-whoever-he-is!"

"You will like Pierre. I have written and asked him to come here." The Comtesse sighed. "I will wait until he does before I decide what to do."

Embarrassed, Miranda sauntered to the window. She had expected her visit to bring some emotional complications, but she had not envisaged the ones now facing her. It was going to be hard to make her grandmother see that one could not turn back the clock, not inculcate a sense of family pride into someone who had grown up without it. "Ask Pierre what you should do," she said. "He's more a Chambray than I am."

"He is not!" There was a flash of fire in the brown eyes. "Pierre's a Chambray by name – you are one by birth!" The thin chest palpitated painfully. "I understand your feelings, but you are not to talk that way."

Miranda ran across the room and knelt by her grandmother's side. "I didn't want to upset you, Grand'mère. What I meant is that we should discuss it with Pierre when he comes. I'm sure *he*'ll know what's the best thing for you to do."

"It's *your* decision too," the old lady reiterated. "Why must you be so obstinate?"

"I can't help it," Miranda said drily. "After all, I'm your granddaughter!"

CHAPTER THREE

MORE quickly than she had believed possible, Miranda settled down to a leisurely pace of living. Awakened at eight-thirty by a maid with her breakfast, she wandered downstairs by ten o'clock and spent the rest of the morning exploring the countryside, making sure she was back at the chateau by noon to greet her grandmother, who rarely appeared before then.

Luncheon was served at twelve-thirty, and afterwards they relaxed in the shade of the terrace, not waking up until tea and lemon was served at four o'clock. By the time dinner was served the sun had taken its toll of Miranda's energy, and she was more than ready for bed when her grandmother retired at nine.

She was horrified at the ease with which she slipped into the life of a lotus-eater. The excitement of her days with Mr. Joseph seemed as though they had never existed, and her plans for the future – so strong in her mind when she had arrived here – were already blurring at the edges.

One week more, Miranda decided on her tenth day at the chateau, and she must return to England.

"I was hoping you would stay for several months," her grandmother said heavily, when she was told.

"I can't go on being idle. I have work to do."

"It is interesting that you should have this flair for design. Your mother had an excellent eye for colour."

"I wish I could remember her clearly," Miranda said. "She seems so pale and ghostly to me."

"She was already dying when you were old enough to remember her."

The Comtesse's voice was ice-cold, and though no mention was made of Roger Dixon, the very omission was significant.

25

A week ago Miranda would have talked of something else, but to do so today smacked of dishonesty.

"It's wrong to blame my father for my mother's death. It could just as easily have happened if she'd gone on living here."

"You speak from ignorance," came the harsh reply. "In Louise's time the only way to fight her illness was to live in a warm, dry atmosphere. Yet because of your father, she settled in a climate that was bound to kill her!"

"Mother made the choice herself. Why do you persist in seeing her as a silly girl without a mind of her own?"

"Because she was! You shouldn't judge her on the things your father has told you about her."

"I'm judging her on the things *you've* said! Since I've been here you've kept telling me how like her I am. Not only in looks, but in what I say and do. If that's true, I'm not surprised she decided to lead a proper life – even for only a few years – than spend a lifetime as an invalid."

"Are you suggesting I *wanted* Louise to be an invalid?"

"Didn't you?"

There was a long silence, punctuated at last by a quivering sigh. "I wanted her to live as long as possible. Was that wrong?"

"Of course not," Miranda said gently. "But she preferred five happy years to thirty lonely ones."

"I realise that now."

Miranda caught the bony hand resting on the cashmere blanket. "It must be awful knowing you were wrong and not being able to do anything about it."

"That is why I found the courage to write to you. Time isn't on my side and I have to make my peace with those I've wronged."

"Just because you look like a granny," Miranda said with determined humour, "there's no need to talk like one! You're going to live for years yet."

The words were like a wave of cold water on a sea of Viennese *schmaltz*, and for an instant the Comtesse sat stunned.

"You're not offended, are you?" Miranda asked anxiously.

"No, no. And please don't undo the good work by apologising!" The old lady struggled to her feet and put her hand in Miranda's strong one. "Our talk has tired me more than I realised. I will go to my room."

Hiding her dismay at the fluctuating colour in her grandmother's cheeks, Miranda escorted her to the large bedroom overlooking the drive. Simone – who seemed to have ears like antennae – was already there and immediately took charge, making Miranda feel in the way.

"Come back and see me when I'm settled," the Comtesse whispered.

"You should sleep and not talk any more," Simone interrupted.

"I'll have plenty of time for sleeping when Miranda returns to England." The voice was gentle, but the brown eyes flashed, and the old servant contented herself by muttering unintelligibly beneath her breath.

Miranda left the bedroom and waited out in the gallery. Even at night, with only a few lamps to cast faint light over the grey stone walls, one had no feeling of gloom. It was a house that had been loved, and she was saddened to think that on her grandmother's death it would also cease to function as a home. Unless of course the unknown Pierre decided to live here. She herself could never afford to do so; nor would she have the time.

Her thoughts raced into the future. If she became successful she might be able to make the chateau her home; her very own castle in Provence, in whose tranquillity she could rest and design her new collections!

Pushing aside the fantasy, she pondered on what she had learned this evening. In refusing to see her daughter after her runaway marriage the Comtesse had hurt no one except herself, for by the time she had repented her behaviour it had been too late to make amends: her daughter was dead. The hope that her granddaughter would appease her conscience had been doomed at their first meeting when Miranda – faced with an autocratic, elderly stranger – had burst into a storm of tears and run from the room. Small wonder that her grandmother had returned to France and not contacted her again; might never have done so had Alain Maury not offered to buy the Chambray land. Only then did pride in her heritage decide the Comtesse to offer her granddaughter the chance of retaining the family home – something that would be easy to do once they had Maury money.

Miranda walked along the gallery. Even with money to maintain the chateau she could never live in it. It was a home for a family and deserved more than being used as a weekend retreat from London or Paris. If Pierre Chambray did not want it either, then her grandmother should accept Alain Maury's offer to buy it with the land; at least then it would remain intact.

Miranda was filled with sadness. If only she could have shared her childhood with the frail but proud old lady she was beginning to know and love. How much they would have gained from each other. She glanced down into the hall, savouring the faintly musty odour of brocade and tapestry, the resinous smell of wood lovingly polished over the centuries. What a deep sense of security there was in having a background like this. Yet her mother had left it all for love. Perhaps the very strength of her heritage had given her the strength to leave it.

Would she herself have such strength? It was difficult to know, for she had never been in love. Never had time for it, in fact. Unaccountably she felt a pang of regret. Her work might suffice for a time, but it would be wrong to let it become her only way of life.

What was stopping her from remaining at the chateau and preparing the designs for her new collection? Where else would she find such peace and tranquillity: a library to work in, her every need catered for and a beautiful landscape to give her peace of mind.

"The Comtesse will see you now." Simone stood in the gallery, her face as long and dark as her dress.

With a murmur Miranda went into the bedroom to tell her grandmother of her decision.

"I can't believe it!" the Comtesse sighed happily. "It is what I have prayed for. Now we can really get to know each other."

Having made her decision, Miranda was surprised at how contented she felt. It was as if, from the moment of her arrival, the chateau had laid hands on her heart. Brought up in a London flat, surrounded by neighbours who came and went, she was astonished that bricks and mortar could mean so much to her.

She wrote immediately to tell her father of her change of plans.

"I'll come home when I've finished my designs. Then I'll hire a workroom, a couple of models and someone to help me make up the clothes. But I'll certainly be staying on for the next six weeks. You've no idea how wonderful it is here. Mother must have loved you very much to leave this place."

Within a few days an answering letter came from her father, enclosing an enormous bundle of fabric samples for next spring which several manufacturers had sent her. Ridiculous to think that this April she was looking at materials for next year.

"How many clothes are you going to make?" her grandmother questioned, looking with interest at the swatches on Miranda's lap.

"About twenty. That's as much as I can afford. And don't offer to help me, because I'll refuse."

"It's not shameful to accept help. There would be no strings attached to it."

"I know. But unfortunately I'd supply my own!"

Miranda stood up and dumped the samples on to the chair. Rummaging in the pocket of her yellow dress, she found a matching ribbon and tied her long, honey-gold hair away from her face. It made her look like one of Wordsworth's daffodils. "Working here is going to be like an extended holiday."

"May I see your sketches — or do you like to keep them secret?"

"I've no secrets from you," Miranda smiled. "Besides, for a little old lady living in the country you've got a keen eye for fashion!"

"When Louise was young we bought our clothes in Paris — we could afford it then."

Talk of clothes overcame the discretion which had kept Miranda's curiosity quiet since her arrival here. "Were you very rich at one time?"

"Rich enough not to think about money! Henri — your grandfather — never discussed it with me. It wasn't until he died — when Louise was seventeen — that I discovered we'd been living on capital, and that there wasn't much of *that* left either!"

"It must have been a shock."

"I managed."

Indomitable spirit came through in the two words, giving Miranda a clear picture of the penny-pinching that must have taken place in order to conserve money without altering appearances.

"At least you never thought my father was a fortune-hunter," she said, and instantly wished the words unspoken, for her grandmother's expression grew sad.

"I *never* doubted his love for Louise. I just used to pray he loved her enough to leave her. It's only in recent months that I realised that even if he *had* gone away, she would have followed him."

A faint sigh concluded the words, and glancing at her watch,

Miranda saw it was three o'clock. "You're missing your afternoon nap. Have a rest and I'll come back later."

The Comtesse was about to reply when the telephone rang. Simone could be heard answering it, and a moment later she padded in carrying the receiver extension.

"Monsieur Chambray is calling from Paris," she muttered, and plugged the telephone into the wall.

Uncertain whether to go or stay, Miranda hovered by the door until her grandmother fluttered her hand towards a chair. Quietly she sat down, listening to the one-sided conversation.

At first the Comtesse seemed angry as she answered questions and asked several herself. But as the call continued, her voice softened, and by the time it came to an end she was smiling.

"Pierre rang to apologise for not replying to my letter. But he was in America and only came back last night. He will be coming down at the weekend to meet you."

"It's a long way to come just to see *me*," Miranda murmured.

"There will be much to talk over," the Comtesse said. "The future of the Chambray estate rests with you both."

"Sorry, Grand'mère," Miranda said hastily, and stood up. "Now have your nap. I'll be back for tea."

"I didn't think you'd be back to see *me*!"

With a soft laugh Miranda touched her fingers to the bony cheek, then walked through the open French windows to the terrace.

It was difficult to believe that in England the skies were grey and people were still wearing woollens. Here the temperature was in the high sixties, and the azaleas bordering the lawn were a riot of colour. The sun blazed down from an electric blue sky yet the air was still clear and faintly moist. Did it ever have the dry aridness depicted in so many of Cézanne's paintings, she wondered, or did the streams that flowed down from the mountain ranges keep this area of Provence moist and lush?

She set off across the grass, her steps making no sound on the springy turf. Maurice, whom she had glimpsed once or twice since her arrival, spent a good part of each day tending the grounds in sight of the chateau windows, but even this barely kept the weeds at bay. He made no attempt to do anything with the land that could not be seen by the Comtesse's vigilant eye, and the further Miranda walked the more she felt she was entering a landscape untouched by hand.

No sound broke the stillness of the day; neither a droning insect nor a bird, and it was not till she had been walking for some half-hour that the chatter of water came to her ears. The ground had begun to slope sharply and she was not sure if she was still on Chambray property. Several large boulders and many small rocks lay scattered around, and she picked her way carefully past them. The descent was steeper than she had imagined, and the lower she went the cooler the air became.

Coming round a bend in the path she found herself on a flat ridge of land that dropped down in a terrifying rush to a narrow gorge where water roared along on its headlong flight from the distant mountains. Careful not to lose her footing, she walked to the edge and peered over.

She had to look a long way down.

Several hundred yards below, the water dashed itself against the huge boulders that lay tumbled on the river bed, spuming and foaming in fury to find its path even partially blocked. Moving her eyes from the angry water, she studied the land on the far side. Small areas of the mountainside appeared to be cultivated, and she guessed there must be several paths leading down to the valley. But there were none she easily saw, and unwilling to continue with her exploration, she turned to go back.

A flash of blue caught her eye and she swung round to look at it. Further along the edge, almost hidden by a stunted tree that jutted out from the sparse earth, a small rose bush triumphantly flourished.

32

With a cry of pleasure she ran forward to look at it, her amazement growing as she saw several buds and some half-opened flowers. It was incredible that a rose bush should be flourishing at this time of year. She bent to examine it, savouring the heady perfume. No wonder Monsieur Maury had spent years trying to perfect it!

Carefully she pulled off several of the opened flowers – it was a shame to leave them here to die unseen – and cradling them in her arms, she scrambled back up the sharp incline to the more gently sloping land.

Skirting the terrace, she went through the kitchen garden – where herbs stood in neat little rows like sentries – to the large, old-fashioned kitchen that cried out for ten servants and now had to be satisfied with one. Miranda found a plain white china bowl and arranged the flowers in them, so intent on what she was doing that she was unaware of someone watching her until she looked up and saw Simone's dark, baleful eyes.

"I found these on the mountain," Miranda explained. "I thought my grandmother would like them."

"She will like anything you bring her," the old housekeeper said, her voice thin with dislike. "Having you here has given her great happiness. But what will happen when you go?"

"I'm not going yet. I'll be here for at least two months."

"That will only make it worse when you *do* leave! It is wrong of you to stay. Wrong and thoughtless!"

"It is not your business to question what I do."

"It is my business to look after the Comtesse – the way I've looked after her since your mother ran off and left her! The way *you* will leave her when you've finished using her!"

At last the woman's fears were disclosed; the reason for her dislike openly stated. Knowing it was not jealousy but the anger of genuine concern, Miranda's own dislike of her faded.

"Even when I go back to England, I intend to come and see my grandmother as often as I can."

"You say that now – while you're here – but once you have

33

gone you will forget her!"

"Wait and see," Miranda replied, and picking up the bowl of roses, walked out.

The front door was open, as it usually was at this time of day, and sunlight streamed into the hall, falling across one wall like a bar of gold and catching Miranda's hair as she skirted the side of the staircase.

The man coming in through the door stopped with a strangled sound. Hearing it, Miranda turned and saw a thin, serious-looking young man in a dark suit. His tanned face was unsmiling and his amber brown eyes were watching her intently.

"So we meet again," he said.

"I'm afraid I don't –" Miranda said, and then did, stopping with a gasp as she recognised the insufferably rude man she had met at the airport. "What are *you* doing here?"

"I have called to see the Comtesse."

If he was curious about her own presence he hid it remarkably well, and ignoring her, knocked on the door of the salon and went in.

Miranda heard her grandmother greet him warmly, and wondering unhappily who he could be, she followed him inside.

"I'd like you to meet Alain Maury," her grandmother said. "Alain, this is my granddaughter, Miranda Dixon."

So this was the propagator of the blue rose! Setting down the bowl she was carrying, Miranda made a pretence of re-arranging the flowers; anything was better than having to face the man whose eyes she could feel boring into her back.

"My granddaughter was most intrigued by the story," the Comtesse continued. "She thought it highly romantic."

Miranda swung round before her grandmother could say any more. "Did you discover the rose by accident, *monsieur*?"

"It took me three years to produce a hardy strain."

"But without a scent?"

34

"Without a scent," he conceded, "until I discovered it would grow on *this* land."

Miranda crossed to a chair and sat down, wishing she was wearing something more sophisticated than yellow cotton. Having regarded her green suit as a ridiculous get-up, he would no doubt find this simple dress more suited to his unsophisticated taste. Not that he himself looked particularly unsophisticated, she thought, studying him from beneath her lashes; for at close quarters his manner was aloof and his features as well cut as his navy jacket. Not an easy man to know, she surmised, seeing temper in the nervous flaring of his nostrils and impatience the twitch of his thin but well-shaped mouth. Too well shaped, she thought; there was something almost effeminate in its curve. Not effeminate, she amended quickly as, aware of her regard, he stared back at her. There was too much steel in his character for that.

"I have told Miranda you wish to buy my land," the Comtesse was saying, "but I cannot give you an answer until she and Pierre have talked it over."

"Indeed?" The tenseness of the man's body belied the unconcern of his voice. "I was under the impression that Pierre had made his home in Paris."

"He has. But if Miranda wished to live here . . ."

Miranda stirred restlessly, wondering if her grandmother was deliberately trying to forget that she had already turned down this suggestion. But before she could speak, the man had swung round to face her, his amber-coloured eyes gleaming like topaz in his dark face.

"I had heard that you were here only for a holiday, Miss Dixon. The land can mean nothing to you."

"It's Chambray land," she said coldly, determined that though she would eventually concede he was right, she would at least make him sweat a little.

"But you can have no use for it," he insisted. "And I have told the Comtesse I am willing to increase my offer."

"I will discuss it with Pierre. He will be here this weekend."

Alain Maury looked at the Comtesse. "I will come and see you next week if I may."

"Miranda will call you," the Comtesse said, extending her hand.

Alain Maury raised the bony fingers to his lips. The old-fashioned gesture became him surprisingly well, turning his superciliousness into courtliness.

"*Mademoiselle*." Amber eyes, no longer solicitous but hard as agate, looked at Miranda. "I hope your stay here is a pleasant one." With a final bow in the Comtesse's direction, he walked out.

Not until his footsteps had died away did Miranda feel free to speak.

"So that's Alain Maury! Do you remember my telling you about that rude man at the airport?"

"Not Alain?" The Comtesse gave a laugh. "So I wasn't wrong in sensing sparks between you. But I had the feeling it was caused by something more than a disputed taxi."

"Taxis can be important when you want one," Miranda said, "and he was livid with me for getting to the rank first."

"His humour is not of the best," the Comtesse acknowledged. "He has never recovered from Lucille's death."

"He was married?" Miranda was surprised that any girl could have been foolish enough to fall in love with him.

"He was engaged," came the correction. "A month before his marriage Lucille fell to her death on the mountain – near the ledge where you found these roses."

Despite herself, Miranda felt shock. "Was Monsieur Maury with her?"

"No. He was in Grasse. She had gone walking on her own. I am rather hazy about the details, but as you can imagine, the tragedy affected him deeply."

Miranda was silent. The death of his fiancée might well have affected the Frenchman, yet she doubted if he had been

36

an easy man to get on with even before it had happened. His arrogance was inbred, and though in another person tragedy might have had a softening effect, with him it had had the exact opposite.

But she must not allow her dislike of him to motivate her behaviour. If he wished to buy this land she had no right to prevent him.

"If you are satisfied that he has offered you a good price," she said firmly, "you should sell."

"The chateau as well?" the Comtesse asked faintly.

Miranda hesitated and then decided that bluntness was less cruel than the raising of false hopes. "The house as well – unless Pierre wants to live here. *I* would never be able to."

"When you spoke to Alain I had the impression you had changed your mind about leaving here."

"I did it to annoy Monsieur Maury."

"I see," the Comtesse said again. "I hadn't appreciated that you disliked him so much."

"Neither had I until I saw him again," Miranda said slowly. "But I don't think I've met anyone I've disliked more!"

CHAPTER FOUR

IN a bright red sports car as exuberant and dashing as its owner, Pierre Chambray arrived at the chateau late on Friday afternoon.

In her bedroom, where she had gone to read a book on fashion which she had discovered in the library, Miranda heard him mount the stairs, his voice amused as he teased Simone.

Excited at the prospect of meeting another member of the family, she decided to wear one of her more sophisticated dresses that night. First impressions were important and she was determined to show this man that she was too sophisticated to succumb to her grandmother's matchmaking; that this was in the Comtesse's mind had become increasingly obvious in the last few days. Pierre had undoubtedly been given all *her* vital statistics and character outline too – and she was going to make it clear that she had every intention of remaining her own mistress. Certainly never mistress or wife to a Frenchman!

Alain Maury's face flashed into her mind, and she tugged a comb furiously through her hair. What on earth had made her suddenly think of him?

Opening the wardrobe, she debated between black crepe and geranium jersey. The jersey won and she zipped herself inside its clinging folds and clasped a wide, tightly-fitting band of glittering jet around her waist. To suit the almost mediaeval simplicity of the dress, she brushed her hair into a pageboy, the ends curving towards her chin and emphasising her high cheekbones and the delicate planes of her face.

It was the first time since her arrival that she had worn a long dress, and the skirts floated behind her as she went down the stairs, making her feel like a chatelaine in her very own castle. As indeed it could be if she said the word. Quickly she pushed the tempting thought aside and went into the salon.

The Comtesse had also dressed for the occasion, her usual pastel wool replaced by black taffeta, with a sparkle of diamonds at her ears and throat. But it was the man standing beside her who commanded Miranda's attention, for he looked more like an explorer than the advertising executive she knew him to be. He was tall, broad and blond, with freckles spattering a wide forehead and reddish-blond brows marking the palest of blue eyes. His nose and mouth were large, as were his hands which reached out and caught hers in a warm clasp.

"So you're Miranda." His voice suited his appearance, being deep and reverberating. "Admirably named, I may say. I can see why Tante Emilie was so insistent about my coming here."

"I'm glad we can meet," Miranda replied. "After all, we're the only Chambrays left."

"A saddening thought. At the turn of the century there were at least fifty."

She was surprised. "What happened to them?"

"More daughters than sons – and two wars, of course. I'm the last male in the line." He grinned. "I try not to think of it, but every time I come here Tante Emilie reminds me of it."

"It hasn't done much good," the Comtesse commented.

The man's reply was forestalled by Simone who came in to announce dinner, and Pierre escorted his aunt to the dining room.

He displayed the same deferential attitude towards her as Alain Maury, though he was more humorous with it. This might have been because he was a member of the family. The French were sticklers for etiquette, Miranda knew, and no stranger would have dared tease the Comtesse the way Pierre was doing.

As always, dinner was excellent, and Pierre made appreciative noises at every course, particularly at the superb claret. "Is the Latour in honour of Miranda's presence or mine?"

"It honours you both," the Comtesse said. "You are of equal importance to me."

He relaxed visibly at the words, and Miranda wondered if he had been afraid that her own presence here would affect an inheritance he had always regarded as his own. Not that there was all that much to inherit. A decaying chateau too big to be used as anything other than an institution or school, and acres of barren land that had only acquired value because of their use to Alain Maury.

Alain Maury. What a difference he could make to their lives!

Coffee was served in the salon, and Pierre entertained them with a racy account of his stay in America.

"Do you have many clients there?" Miranda asked.

"The one I got is the first. Two other agencies were competing for the business, but we got it because we were French."

"Then the client's either in perfume or fashion!"

"Fashion," he grinned. "They have three hundred stores and are planning to open up in Europe."

"Do you know much about fashion?" she asked.

"For a million dollars' account I'll learn!"

"That sounds rather — most expedient," the Comtesse chided.

"Business *is* expedient." Pierre Chambray was lighting a cigarette, and he paused with a match in his hand. "Believe me, Tante Emilie, it doesn't matter whether you're making tractors, selling groceries or working on the Bourse; once you're dealing with people for profit, you have to watch out for the main chance!"

"You sound as if you've no ideals at all," Miranda could not help saying.

"Ideals and making a lot of money are not good bed companions!" His smile was sly. "Excuse the metaphor, but I'm French!"

She smiled back. "I still think it's possible to be a success

40

and keep your principles."

"In a profession maybe. Not in business."

"Alain is a man of principle." The Comtesse entered the conversation, though her remark seemed momentarily to end it, for there was a long silence.

"Alain's in a different category," Pierre said at last. "He may not be unscrupulous in monetary terms, but he is as far as his emotions are concerned. He puts business before everything else. If he didn't, Lucille would still be alive today."

"You're repeating gossip," the Comtesse reproved. "You should know better than that."

"Forgive me. But you will at least admit that when it comes to business, Alain knows what he's doing."

"He is extremely successful," the Comtesse agreed, "but he is honest."

Pierre grunted, but the look he cast Miranda spoke volumes.

"We must discuss the land," the Comtesse said suddenly. "It is one of the reasons for you being here."

"I thought you had agreed to sell," he said sharply.

"Not quite. I wish to make sure that neither you nor Miranda will regret it if I do."

"The land's going to waste," he replied firmly. "Far better to sell it to someone who can use it." Aware that he had spoken before Miranda had been given a chance to reply, he looked at her apologetically. "I take it you agree with me?"

"Yes."

"There you are, then!" Pierre said to his great-aunt. "Accept the offer and go on a spending spree!"

The Comtesse folded her hands in her lap. "It is a considerable amount of money. Alain telephoned me tonight, and doubled his offer!"

For the first time that evening Pierre was speechless, and enjoying the sensation she had caused, the Comtesse went on: "You can thank Miranda for *that*. She gave him the impression she didn't want to sell the land. That's why he increased the price – providing I confirm the arrangement before the weekend is over."

Pierre turned a respectful look on Miranda. "When it comes to business tactics, you don't do so badly yourself!"

"It was unintentional," Miranda said hastily. "Monsieur Maury got the idea I wanted to live here."

"Don't apologise for what you did," Pierre said exultantly, and swung round to his aunt. "This land must be more important to him than I'd realised. Are you sure he only wants it for flower farming? He could buy thousands of hectares round here without doubling his offer to *you*."

"He needs the land in the valley," Miranda intervened. "Don't you know?"

"Know what?"

Miranda looked at her grandmother. "I'm sorry, Grand'-mère, I thought Pierre had been told."

"I didn't do so because I was anxious to avoid –" The Comtesse hesitated, then said: "Anxious not to have the sale of my land turned into an auction."

"An auction!" Pierre looked angry. "Good heavens, Tante Emilie, what's the matter with you? You've been struggling over money for years and when you get the chance of making some . . . If you would kindly tell me the whole story . . ."

"Those blue roses," the Comtesse said, pointing to the flowers whose heady perfume filled the room, "cannot be grown with a scent anywhere else except on my land."

"*Enfin!*" Pierre's breath expelled on a sigh. "At last it makes sense! No wonder he doubled his offer. We must think carefully before we accept it. We might be able to make him go higher yet."

"There's a market price for everything," the Comtesse reproved. "Alain is no fool. He knows what the land is worth."

"He's already offered you double what it's worth! Everyone up here has land for sale, and it's likely to be that way for the next hundred years. It's only because of these flowers of his that *this* land is important to him. I wish you'd told me about it before. Still, you haven't signed anything, so it's not too late." Pierre was pacing the floor and not bothering to hide his excitement. "It's a good thing Miranda arrived when she did, otherwise you'd have given him the land for a song."

"Alain is our neighbour," the Comtesse said quietly. "I have no intention of holding him to ransom."

A wary look came over Pierre's face. "Think what a difference the extra money would make to the chateau," he said softly. "Neither Miranda nor I could afford to run it the way our finances are now. But with Alain's offer. . . . Don't you see what it means? We could afford to keep the chateau and make it as magnificent as it used to be!"

"You – you always said you preferred to – to – live in Paris," the Comtesse faltered.

"Because I can't earn a living anywhere else! But do you think I *want* you to sell the chateau? I'm a Chambray, Tante Emilie – this place is part of my heritage!"

"You never gave me that impression."

"I was trying to pretend I didn't care."

Colour came and went in the lined face and with an effort the Comtesse composed herself. "You young people are so adept at hiding your feelings . . . Sometimes it is difficult to believe you have any."

"It often requires money," Pierre replied drily, "to indulge in your feelings, and that's something we've always been short of."

"And if we had the money – would you be willing to live here?"

"Certainly." The reply was loud and clear. "But Miranda takes precedence over me, Tante Emilie. She is your granddaughter."

"My home is in England," Miranda said quickly.

"My estate will be divided between both of you," the Com-

43

tesse said imperiously.

"Please don't talk about it!" Miranda cried, putting her arms round her grandmother's shoulders. "You'll live for years yet. I want you to spend the money on yourself."

"I want it for the house."

"Then spend it on the house and enjoy living in it! But for goodness' sake stop talking about leaving your money to us." She glanced at Pierre. "Do you agree with me?"

"Without question. We French are inclined to be too practical. It leads to morbidity!" Bending over his aunt, he swung her into his arms. "You must go to bed. In the morning I will go to Grasse and talk to a few people I know. I want to find out what makes these roses *so* important to Alain."

"Their scent," Miranda put in. "It's out of this world!"

"That shows how poor my nose is!" Pierre laughed and, striding over to the door, pushed it open with his foot. "Don't disappear, Miranda," he called over his shoulder. "I'll be back to talk to you."

Left alone, Miranda thought about her newly met cousin. Even if the sale of the land brought sufficient money to restore the chateau to its former glory, she could not envisage him leaving Paris to live here. Though she had only just met him she was positive his only interest was in the money itself.

She ran her hand over the marble mantelpiece. At least he had the kindness not to let his aunt know he did not share her love for the chateau. What would its future be? A finishing school for rich socialites or an orphanage? She shook her head. It was too isolated to be practical for either.

"What deep thoughts are you thinking?" Pierre had returned, as quiet as a panther, giving her no chance to compose her face.

"Just that you're not the type to settle down in the country," she replied bluntly. "You'll be in a fix if Grand'mère leaves you this place."

"*You* are closer kin than I am!"

"I don't want anything from my grandmother," Miranda said vehemently.

"She has already made her plans. You won't be able to stop her. If Alain buys the land there'll be a lot of money involved. At least half a million francs. Maybe double before we're finished."

"You're not going to ask for *more*?"

"Who knows? I'll decide when I've been to Grasse."

"And spoken to your spies?"

"My contacts," he smiled. "It always pays to have contacts." He walked over to the sideboard. "Care for a brandy?"

"No, thanks." She watched as he poured one for himself and returned to sit in a chair in front of her.

In repose he was older than she had first imagined, at least thirty-six, with an experienced face that added to his attraction, as did the cynicism that touched his mouth. Here was no callow youth but a man of the world who knew the worth of his charm and would not hesitate to use it.

She considered his remarks about Alain Maury. The pleasure of annoying the young Frenchman was beginning to wear thin, and what had begun as an impulse earlier this afternoon was now developing into a deliberate business ploy that she found distasteful. Worse still, she could almost feel sorry for Alain, whose only desire was to grow his wonderful roses.

"I think there's something nice about using land for flowers," she said. "Flowers and food — that's what land is all about."

"And houses and schools and roads!" He sipped his brandy. "Don't tell me you're a romantic?"

"Half the time!"

"Which half of you designs clothes?"

"Both halves," she smiled.

"I've been told you're very talented."

"Don't believe everything Grand'mère says."

"She has told me nothing. I heard it from some friends in London."

"Your contacts?" she asked drily.

"My spies!" he laughed. "They say you'll go to the top."

"Only if I'm lucky."

"Success is all around you," he said confidently. "I sensed it the moment we met." He flexed his hands. "I admire success more than anything in the world."

She remembered the dashing red sports car parked in the drive. "You haven't done so badly yourself."

"A small salary and a big expense account. In terms of real money I'm a non-starter." There was unexpected bitterness in his voice. "I was brought up to believe that being a Chambray was the greatest thing that could happen to you, and I was eighteen before I realised that money in the bank – even if it had only been there a few weeks – meant more than a name that had been with you for generations!"

"Most people start their careers without money," Miranda retorted, "and without a family name either. Take Madame Maury – she began with nothing."

Pierre grinned. "You've put me in my place, *chérie*! From now on I won't complain."

She decided to change the subject. "Have you known Alain Maury long?"

"Since he was thirteen. That's when he moved here. I was already living at the chateau with my mother and he used to follow me round like a puppy. Success changed him for the worse. It often does."

"I thought you admired success?"

"Only if it comes from talent. And his comes from a lust for power. That's all he cares about!"

"It's understandable in a way," she murmured. "The girl he loves is dead and –"

"He killed her," Pierre said. "He killed her as surely as if he'd pushed her over the ridge!" Miranda stared at him in

46

astonishment, and seeing it, he shrugged. "I thought you knew?"

"Grand'mère said it was an accident — that she fell."

"She jumped. There's no doubt of it. And Alain blames himself. There's no doubt of *that* either."

"Did he say so?"

"Words weren't necessary. From the day Lucille died he acted as though she'd never existed! She was living at his house at the time, and before the funeral had taken place he had her clothes packed and sent to the poorhouse! He wanted nothing left to remind him of her."

"Grief makes people act strangely."

"It was strange enough to attract comment."

"Villages are notorious for rumours."

"The police made enquiries," Pierre said casually.

"The local constable trying to keep the gossip quiet, I suppose," she said scornfully.

"A member of the Sûreté," Pierre corrected.

Miranda swallowed her discomfiture. "Did you know the girl?" she asked.

"Of course. She was Madame Maury's goddaughter. She knew Alain since they were children and was in love with him for years. But he didn't want to settle down. It was only because of his mother's insistence that he agreed to do so." Pierre frowned. "He changed his mind again a month before the wedding and she couldn't face being jilted. So she killed herself."

The matter-of-fact way in which Pierre spoke only served to heighten the poignancy of his words.

"What a waste of a life," Miranda whispered.

"I agree. That's why your sympathy for Alain is unwarranted. He has an adding machine where his heart should be."

"He's made some wonderful perfumes," she remarked.

"He's got a nose for business!" Pierre quipped. "And we

47

must have the same. I'm sure we can get him to increase his offer for the land."

Pity for the unknown Lucille destroyed Miranda's earlier sympathy for Alain Maury. "See what you can find out in Grasse. Then we can decide."

"Good." He stood up. "Shall I carry *you* to your room?"

She laughed and with a twirl of skirts preceded him to the hall. Together they went up the staircase, pausing at the top to look down at the hall.

"I love this place," she murmured. "I never thought bricks and mortar could mean so much to me in such a short time."

"You're more of a Chambray than I am," Pierre said lightly. "I wouldn't care if I never saw it again."

"What will you do if Grand'mère leaves it to you?"

"Retain it if there's enough money to do so, and hope you'll come and share it with me!"

His words made her look at him. In the dim light his eyes were in shadow and his expression difficult to read. The lift at the corners of his mouth could have been tenderness or humour. Deciding to ignore the comment, she walked to her room. Pierre followed her and leaned against the wall as she opened her door.

"I hope I won't wake up tomorrow and find you have disappeared," he said.

"You can always find me in the library," she laughed. "I work better there than anywhere else."

"Work?" he asked.

"I'm designing a collection. I hope to start up on my own."

"You should try and persuade Alain to give you the blue rose scent. If you launched your own perfume as well as your own clothes you'd be in the money right away."

"I'd need a stack of money to do it," she retorted. "But I'll bear it in mind for the future — if I don't end up back in wholesale again!"

"You won't," he prophesied. "I feel it in my bones."

"What else do your bones tell you?"

"Many things." He caught her hand and raised it to his lips, his eyes mocking yet tender. "Many things."

CHAPTER FIVE

TIRED though she was, Miranda did not sleep well that night. What she had learned of Alain Maury returned to haunt her dreams and she awoke at six o'clock, heavy-eyed and listless.

Padding over to the window, she opened the wooden shutters, already warm from the sun, though the air that flowed over her shoulders held the cool of dawn. This was the loveliest time of day: the grass glittering with dew, the moisture in the air intensifying the colours of the landscape: greening the leaves, browning the earth and making the sky seem a deeper, more vivid blue.

In the pristine light of early morning the dark tragedy of Lucille was already fading. Perhaps it had been the way Pierre had told the story – his every remark about Alain filled with dislike – that had made her feel as if Lucille's unhappiness had been her own personal one. But now she no longer felt it. Alain Maury's past had nothing to do with her and she must forget it.

It was barely seven when she went downstairs, and quietness lay like a shroud in all the rooms. She went into the kitchen to make breakfast: a jug of creamy milk taken from the large can left at the back door several hours ago by a farmer, a wedge of yellow butter, crisp golden biscottes – she was too hungry to wait for the warm croissants to arrive from the village – and a jar of home-made apricot jam with the tang of lemon and a subtle taste of fresh almonds.

All this, together with a pot of fragrant coffee, she carried out to the terrace, where the early morning sun was just appearing to warm the tiled floor. Basking in the rays, she began to eat. Around her the landscape was coming to life; a breeze stirred the pointed heads of the cypresses and ruffled the wide skirts of the olive trees, making the lower leaves dance like flounces on a ball gown. An electric saw whirred in the distance while from near at hand came the bleating of goats as they began their daily wander on the mountainside.

Miranda's tenseness slowly evaporated. There was a magic in this part of Provence that made it impossible for her to be anything other than blissful.

"You look as if you're going to melt into the scenery," a deep voice said, and her cup clattered into her saucer as she looked round and saw Pierre. In tan slacks and a fine-spun silk sweater of that particular shade of blue called French navy, he looked more handsome than she had remembered; his eyes a brighter blue, the faint lines fanning out from them indicating humour as well as experience.

Drawing out a chair, he sat beside her. "What brings *you* down so bright and early?"

"Work," she said, unwilling to tell him of her restless night. "You're no lie-a-bed yourself."

"I'm off to Grasse," he reminded her, and fell silent as Simone appeared with a tray.

The woman's taciturn face creased into a smile as she set it down in front of him, and she muttered to him in clipped French which Miranda could not understand. It was only when he answered, his tone clearer, that she knew they were speaking in the local patois, and it made her realise that for all his world-weary air, he was still a country boy.

"Were you born here?" she asked as Simone went away.

"In Alsace, actually. My father was killed in a mining accident and Tante Emilie invited my mother to make her home here."

"Then you must remember *my* mother."

"Very well." He broke a croissant, buttered it liberally and ate half in one gulp, with the quick, relishing movements so

51

often seen in Frenchmen at table. "Much as I hate to admit it, dear cousin, I'm thirteen years older than you, and I have a great many fond memories of Louise." The smile left his face and his expression grew sombre. "And some sad ones, too. It was a bad time at the chateau when she ran away with your father."

For the first time someone whom she considered outside the family circle was talking about her parents. Though a Chambray, Pierre had been too young to be emotionally involved in what he had seen, and though his opinions might still be clouded by all he had overheard, he had come sufficiently far from the past to have formed a more unbiased opinion of his own.

"Did you know my father too?" she asked diffidently.

"Louise once got him to take us both out to tea." Pierre ate the other half of the croissant and reached for another. "He struck me as a typical Englishman — solid, dependable and smoking a pipe! I've always remembered that pipe. He lit it when we were having tea and it made Louise cough. He put it away immediately."

"I don't think he ever lit it again," Miranda told him. "But he still carries one, and fills it as well!" She hesitated and then said: "Do you think he was wrong to marry my mother? Don't spare my feelings, Pierre."

"I'm always truthful to my partners, *chérie*. It's my one virtue! No, I don't think he was wrong. Besides, if he'd run off to Timbuctoo, Louise would have followed him. Like most placid types she could be extremely obstinate when she wanted, and there was no doubt she wanted your father."

"Thank you for saying that. You don't know how much you've helped me." Miranda pushed back her chair. "I must get on with some work."

"I'll see you when I get back from Grasse."

She walked to the end of the terrace and the open doors of the library. Only as she reached the threshold did she pause and turn back to look at Pierre. "Why did you say I was your partner?"

"Because we're working together in the business of getting a better price from Alain," he laughed, and laughed again as she gave an exclamation and disappeared.

Miranda was seated at the beautiful marquetry desk, her sketch pad open in front of her, when she heard Pierre drive away. Ruefully she looked at the blank sheets. Half an hour and not a single line drawn. Resolutely she set her pencil down on the paper, but it remained motionless, and after a moment she flung it away and stood up.

It did not help to have peace and quiet in which to work, if one did not also have peace of mind; and if Pierre had done nothing else, he had disturbed her sufficiently to make concentration impossible. The past was too alive to be buried, and memories she had thought forgotten were now surfacing to irritate her.

More than ever she deplored the bitterness that had prevented her grandmother from seeing her years ago. How much they would have benefited from each other! Even after a short acquaintance there was an affinity between them that stretched across the difference in their age and upbringing.

Miranda sighed and ran her eyes over the bookshelves. For a small chateau, the library was unusually extensive, though many of the books were still so stiff and new that she doubted if they had ever been opened, let alone read.

To her surprise she had found that many of the books were in disorder, as though they had been taken out and then replaced at random. The dramatic works of Victor Hugo stood side by side with the gossip of Saint-Simon, while the brothers Goncourt were cheek by jowl with Stendhal and the poems of Baudelaire. It made looking for a book a labour of love, and also an exciting treasure hunt, for she had come across a volume of hand-engraved drawings depicting French dress from the sixteenth to the nineteenth century. The publishing house was a Parisian one and the author's name appeared on no other book in the library.

When she had shown it to her grandmother the Comtesse had professed ignorance about it. "I've never been a great reader, I'm afraid. Perhaps Henri – your grandfather – or Louise bought it." The fine brown eyes were curious. "Is it valuable, then?"

"I doubt it. It's mainly that it's very interesting to *me*."

"Then take it back to England with you, my child, and any others you want."

"I wouldn't dream of taking any books. They must remain here – where they belong."

"I wish *you* felt like the books," the Comtesse had sighed, and set about her embroidery again.

Miranda remembered this last remark as she stood fingering one of the leather-bound volumes, and she was saddened at being unable to fulfil the wish. Her eyes roamed the shelf nearest to her, and idly she picked out a Colette novel from where it nestled next to some Théophile Gautier poems. What a mess the books were in! If she had the time she would love to put them in order. Perhaps next year ... But next year – if her collection was a success – she would be too busy to take a holiday. She yawned. How far away the London fashion scene was from this rural backwater and how different the musty peace of this room from the brightly-lit and over-crowded workroom at Mr. Joseph's.

She walked back to the desk and closed her sketch book. She was obviously not in the mood to work this morning, and rather than fight a losing battle she would do better to use the time to complete several errands: post a letter to her father, see if the local newsagent sold felt-tipped pens and replenish her stock of gouache colours.

Collecting her handbag, she set off for the village. Her hair swung against her face as she walked, and she drew out an emerald ribbon from the pocket of her full-skirted dress and pulled her hair back into a ponytail. It made her look no more than sixteen, until one saw the provocative slant of her eyes and the voluptuous curve of her mouth.

The single village street had its usual influx of shoppers, elderly women in long black skirts with laced-up boots and laced-up faces, and younger housewives in cotton dresses or knitted suits; but all had the common denominator of bulging shopping bags. Several opulent cars were packed beside the fountain in the village square while their owners, casual yet well-dressed women of indeterminate age, placed their orders with the butcher or the greengrocer or waited for the arrival of the refrigerated fish-van which came from Cannes to sell them shiny black mussels, grey and coral-spotted shrimps, and the lumpy *loup* – as familiar to the housewife in Provence as cod was to her counterpart in England.

Aware of several pairs of eyes watching her, Miranda crossed the cobbled street to buy some stamps at the *bar tabac* and then entered the newsagent's. But though she found some pens she could not find any gouache.

"You'll only get those in Cannes or Nice," the shopkeeper said, and turned to serve someone else who had come in.

Glancing round, Miranda saw a girl of her own age. That she was French was unmistakable: it was apparent in the neat figure with its small, high breasts and short waist. That she was rich was equally unmistakable, for the short black hair that fell away from the high forehead and curved forward on the narrow, rouged cheeks had been cut by a master hand, as had the beautifully tailored black linen dress and hand-made shoes and bag that shrieked Rome.

Feeling as if she had stepped off a wholesale dress rack, Miranda returned the other girl's cool stare.

"Would you know if there's an artist's shop in Grasse?" she asked.

"I should think there must be." The girl's voice, like her appearance, was careful and controlled, her French perfect and Parisian. "You are English," she added, her face showing its first sign of interest.

But it was a very dispassionate interest, Miranda decided, meeting the steady brown eyes fringed by short, thick lashes that stuck out so straight they gave the eyes a doll-like appearance not echoed either by the aquiline nose or beautifully shaped but thin mouth.

"My accent always gives me away," Miranda smiled.

"It wasn't your accent," came the cool reply, "so much as your tone of voice. All Englishwomen sound like schoolgirls!"

"Mademoiselle is the granddaughter of the Comtesse Chambray," the proprietress interrupted.

The French girl looked momentarily discomfited. "I heard you were here, but I'd formed the impression of a —" she hesitated — "of a different type."

"Don't let appearances fool you," Miranda answered. "What you heard might have been right!"

The brown eyes narrowed like those of a lynx. "But you don't know what I heard."

"You obviously hadn't imagined me as a typical English schoolgirl type!"

"That is certainly true. Quite the contrary, in fact."

The girl picked up a newspaper and went out, giving Miranda a faint nod as she did so.

Miranda followed, and saw the black linen figure entering the *bar tabac*. Parked outside it was a silver-grey Citroën, the latest and most expensive model, and even as she paused beneath the shadow of a plane tree she saw the girl re-emerge from the café and walk towards it. But it was the man beside her who commanded Miranda's attention, for she had not expected to see Alain Maury again so soon.

He was holding a carton of Gauloises under his arm, its blue matching his silk sweater, and as she watched him he took out a cigarette, lit it and then flung the match away. As he did so he raised his eyes and stared directly into hers. Even

56

though she was some distance away she knew he had recognised her, and though she had an illogical desire to turn and run, she realised it would be rude to do so and remained where she was as, with a remark to his companion, he strolled across the road to her side.

"Good morning, *mademoiselle*, so we meet again."

"That's hardly surprising. Bayronne isn't very big."

"Do I detect regret in your voice?"

"Regret?"

"That it is so small that we *should* meet again?"

Staring at him, she saw no humour in his eyes, and knew he had asked the question in all seriousness. What a peculiar man he was, she thought, and tilted her head defiantly.

"I can think of more pleasant things than meeting *you*, *monsieur*. After all, our meetings have hardly been pleasant ones."

"I did not think our second encounter was unpleasant."

"I still remember the first one."

"Surely *I* am the one who should feel annoyed about it? After all, you *did* take my taxi."

She gasped at his effrontery, and taking advantage of her silence he went on: "Would it not be more civilised to pretend our first meeting was at the chateau? One should always be on the best of terms with one's neighbours."

"I'm only a temporary neighbour."

"But you are the Comtesse's granddaughter."

Before Miranda could answer, the French girl had come to stand beside them, placing her hand proprietorially on the man's arm.

"Do come on, Alain. We'll never get to Grasse by eleven."

"I'd like you to meet Miss Dixon first."

"We met at the newsagent's – though we didn't introduce ourselves." The girl held out her hand. "I'm Colette Dinard."

Miranda forced herself to smile, but as she made a move to turn and walk away, Alain Maury spoke again. "Has your grandmother told you that I spoke to her last night and increased my price?"

"Yes."

"I hope you will persuade her to accept my offer – and quickly. If the roses are not planted soon, they will not be ready for next season."

"The decision is entirely my grandmother's," Miranda said steadily. "I am afraid you misjudge my position."

"I know your position very well," he said emphatically. "I am sure your grandmother will do as you wish."

"I have *no* wishes on the subject."

"Then if you are truly unbiased, perhaps you would be good enough to encourage the sale. At least I could put the land to some use, as well as substantially increasing the Comtesse's bank account!"

Miranda dug her hands into the pockets of her skirt. "Some people don't think money is as important as you do, *monsieur*."

"I *never* think about money," he said gravely. "It is only when you have none that it becomes important enough to think about!"

Her cheeks flamed. "The Chambrays may be poor, Monsieur Maury, but they are rich in tradition!"

For an instant he looked taken aback, then his dark brows drew together in a frown. "I did not mean to be rude, *mademoiselle*. You misunderstood me. I was merely stating a fact. When one has all the money one needs, one no longer considers it. I hope you will forgive me for saying so, but it is well known that the Comtesse has been worried about her financial position for years. If you could persuade her to accept my offer she would at least spend the remainder of her life without such problems."

"I have already told you that the decision is my grandmother's," Miranda reiterated. "But if she listens to anyone, it will be Pierre."

"Pierre!" There was no mistaking the anger in the man's

voice, nor the angry way in which he turned his back on her and marched back to the car.

Scarlet-faced, Miranda continued down the street. Behind her she heard Colette Dinard's laugh, and blindly she opened the door of the first shop she came to and went in. Anything to get away from that infuriating couple!

She found herself in the local *pâtisserie* and debated on a choice between buying some hazelnut crescents or a packet of sugared almonds. She decided on the almonds, and was paying for them when the silver-grey Citroën flashed past the window. Package in hand, she stepped back into the street. Her pleasure in the village had evaporated, dispelled by her meeting with a man whom she had disliked at first sight. What bad luck that he had turned out to be their neighbour! It had been bad luck for him too, she acknowledged, for had she not disliked him she might well have persuaded her grandmother to accept his offer for the land.

Even now she knew she would eventually do so, for no amount of prejudice could make her jeopardise the future of those wonderful blue roses. She drew a deep breath, as though the air itself could conjure up the magic of their scent. What a heavenly perfume it would make! No wonder he was so anxious to produce it. She could not blame him for his single-mindedness, for it was a characteristic they had in common, though he probably had more characteristics in common with Colette Dinard.

Was she his fiancée or just a friend? There had been more than an attitude of friendship in the way the thin-fingered white hand had rested on his arm, and there had definitely been possessiveness in the cool voice that had reminded him that they should be on their way. Yet if she had been his fiancée he would have introduced her as such. That meant they were only friends; though she was convinced this was something the French girl intended to change as soon as she could.

The passing windows gave Miranda back her reflection, and

59

seeing her full skirt and ponytail she laughed out loud. Now she understood the remark which Colette Dinard had made to her in the newsagent's. Having heard about her from Alain – who had assuredly been anything other than complimentary – she had not expected Miranda to look like a teenager. More probably like a hard-faced gold-digger with a decidedly garish way of dressing!

So intent was she on her thoughts that she knocked against a woman emerging from a cobbled alleyway.

"I'm so sorry," she apologised. "I didn't see you. My thoughts were miles away."

"So it would seem."

Unthinkingly Miranda had spoken in English, and she was surprised to hear English in reply.

"I hope they were happy thoughts," the woman continued. "You hit me with such force I had the impression you were wishing you were a steamroller!"

"That would be one way of getting rid of my obstacles," Miranda laughed, and looked more closely at her perceptive neighbour.

She was in her early fifties and made no attempt to pretend otherwise. Yet despite her simple wool suit and lack of make-up, she was extraordinarily good-looking, with a wide, curly-shaped mouth, almond-shaped eyes and a flawless skin.

"I'm sorry I turned *you* into one of the obstacles," Miranda apologised again. "I hope I didn't hurt you?"

"Not at all," the woman fell into step beside her. "Are you here on holiday? It's rather early for tourists."

"I'm staying with my grandmother."

"You can't mean . . . you're not the Comtesse Chambray's granddaughter?"

"You have the edge on *me*," Miranda said ruefully, finding it disconcerting to be known without knowing in return.

"I can easily remedy that." The woman held out her hand. "I'm Adrienne Maury. I believe you know my son."

Dismay that this charming woman was the mother of such a disagreeable man kept Miranda quiet.

"You look surprised," Madame Maury said.

"I am. You're not a bit like your son."

"I have the feeling that's meant as a compliment!"

Miranda lowered her eyes. "Was I so obvious?"

"Not more so than Alain," came the amused retort. "You both ruffled each other's feathers!"

Miranda half smiled at the picture it brought to mind: I'd have yellow or green feathers, she thought, but his would be black.

"Stop looking so fierce," Madame Maury said, "and join me for coffee. At my house," she added as Miranda looked towards the *bar tabac*. "Then I will drive you home."

Miranda hesitated. She longed to know more of this charming woman, yet was reluctant to accept the offer in case it meant meeting her son. Yet he was on his way to Grasse, she suddenly remembered.

"Coffee sounds a wonderful idea," she agreed. "I'd be delighted to join you."

Sitting beside Madame Maury in a small white Mini Cooper, they drove out of the village in the opposite direction from the chateau, but turning steadily as they did so, which would, Miranda knew, bring them round in a curving circle to meet the Chambray land at its nearest point to the tall mountain that sheltered the village from Grasse itself.

Massive stone pillars heralded the entrance to the Maury estate; no doubt now of its owners' wealth, for no money had been spared on tending the sweep of lawns that rushed in a tide of green to the smooth walls of an austere but elegant house, with its long line of deep blue shutters. Bougainvillea cascaded like a purple waterfall around the front door, which was open to the warm day and through which lolloped a golden-haired labrador at the sound of their car.

Madame Maury led the way inside. The house was a perfect foil for its chatelaine, with cool tiled floors warmed by richly coloured rugs, and elegant furniture in a mixture of antique and Italian modern. There was a wealth of pictures and sculptures from the elongated figures of Giacometti to the smooth curves of Arp and the abstraction of Barbara Hepworth.

"Alain's taste," Madame Maury said, intercepting Miranda's glance. "I prefer more realism."

The abstract would suit Alain Maury, Miranda decided; not for him the sensuousness of an Epstein or the warmth of a Henry Moore.

She found herself in a small sitting-room off the main salon. This was obviously Madame Maury's retreat, for fashion magazines littered a low table, together with a pile of lavishly illustrated cookery books.

"My vice," the woman laughed, pointing to them. "I collect cookery books the way other women collect diamonds!"

"Less expensive!"

"Alain says it was pure chance that prevented me from cooking cakes instead of cold cream!"

It was Miranda's turn to laugh. "I can't believe it was merely accident that made you famous."

"My dear, I don't consider myself famous!"

"You're a household name."

"You make me sound like a detergent!"

"Nowhere near as polluting! Your cosmetics are wonderful."

"You use them?" Madame Maury looked pleased and Miranda was glad she could truthfully answer yes. "You're the type of girl I had in mind when I brought out my last range."

"Modern Miss?" Miranda asked in surprise.

"Of course. You fit the bill exactly."

"Not in this dress."

"Possibly not – but I've heard about your green suit!"

Miranda sat down quickly. "Your son was very rude about it."

"He was in a temper. When he is, he often says things he doesn't mean."

A maid came in with coffee and biscuits, and not until she had gone did Madame Maury resume speaking. "He was most distressed when he met you at the chateau last week."

"Why?" Miranda asked, knowing full well what the answer would be.

"Because he was afraid you would try and stop him from buying the land."

"That's ridiculous!"

"I hope so. The blue rose means so much to him. It would be a bitter blow if he couldn't cultivate it."

"Why is it so important?"

"Because it will make a magnificent perfume – you must know that for yourself – and also because it's the first one he's created for several years." A shadow crossed the serene face. "It was a great worry to him that he hadn't done so since. . . . Still, now he *has*." The almond-shaped eyes, their warm sherry brown colour so like her son's, saw the look on Miranda's face. "It requires great talent to create a perfume, you know."

"I didn't know," Miranda admitted bluntly. "I imagined you worked out what essences to use and just mixed them up. Perhaps not as simple as that, but –"

"It requires flair and enormous perseverance to develop a new scent," Madame Maury reiterated. "You'd realise it for yourself if you could smell some of the rubbish I've been asked to sell. Alain has the ability to mix one essence with another in a way that will bring out the most unusual bouquet. A great perfume isn't one scent only, you know, it's a subtle blend of many."

"And your son has great subtlety!"

"You two *have* got off on the wrong foot! It's such a pity.

I'm sure you would have liked each other if you had met under different circumstances."

Miranda stiffened, for the words indicated that Alain Maury liked her as little as she liked him.

"My son is on the defensive with women," Madame Maury continued. "That day at the airport he was anxious to get to Grasse quickly. Some blue rose essence had been distilled in the laboratory and he wanted to start blending it when it was at a special temperature He'd timed everything to the split second and he was frightened he'd arrive too late."

"He should have explained," Miranda said lamely.

"It was a lengthy explanation to give while fighting over possession of a taxi!" The curly mouth was definitely smiling now, and Miranda smiled back.

"You make our argument sound very trivial."

"Most arguments are."

The woman poured coffee from a silver pot and handed a cup to Miranda who sniffed the aroma and then sipped.

"This is delicious!"

"Alain blended it."

"Coffee too?"

"If you've a nose, you can blend anything!"

Conversation became more general after this, though Miranda quickly realised she was being adroitly pumped as to her reasons for coming to the chateau and her plans for the future. There was no doubt Madame Maury was anxious for her son to grow his blooms, and since this could only be done on Chambray land, what better way of overcoming any possible obstacles than by charming the Comtesse's granddaughter. Miranda was faintly disappointed. Her liking for her hostess had been so spontaneous that she had foolishly hoped it had been genuinely reciprocated.

"I'm so glad we have finally met," Madame Maury was saying. "I find you very *sympathique* – it is an unusual trait in an English girl."

Miranda said nothing, and felt sherry-brown eyes regarding her quizzically.

"I did not arrange for you to knock into me," the woman chided, the acute perception of her remark belying the languor of her manner. "Nor had I made any plans to meet you. It was pure chance."

"But you used it," Miranda said before she could stop herself. "I don't blame you, of course. I know you're anxious about the perfume and —"

"Not the perfume, my dear — my anxiety is for Alain. If I hadn't found you so understanding I wouldn't have tried to enlist your help. You see, I admit I am trying to do so — but that is only because I find you understanding. My son has great personal unhappiness, and . . ."

"My grandmother told me." Miranda set her cup on the table. "Pierre spoke about it last night, too."

"Pierre knew Alain very well — and Lucille too. But after she died, Alain withdrew from everyone. It was as if he had to remain alone until he had grown another skin."

The words gave Alain Maury another dimension; a deeper more complex character which, while it did not mitigate the things Miranda disliked about him, at least helped her to see them in a more understanding way. Or was this another deliberate tactic to get her sympathy?

"My grandmother is letting Pierre decide about the land," she said. "I'm sure it's just a matter of money."

"I hope you're right. Alain thinks your grandmother might decide to keep the estate intact for you and Pierre."

"I'm leaving Provence in a few months," Miranda said firmly. "The chateau can never be my home."

"Nor Pierre's?"

"He *might* keep it if he has sufficient money, but he could just as easily give it up and never come down here again."

"Perhaps Alain should offer to buy the entire estate."

"No," Miranda said vehemently, "I don't want my grand-

65

mother to know there's any doubt about Pierre making the chateau his home."

"I see. In that case we will say nothing. But you might perhaps mention it to Pierre. It may interest him to know that if we had the land we would also be willing to give him a good price for the chateau – whenever he wishes to sell it."

"That's bribery."

"It's good business!"

"French people talk of nothing else," Miranda sighed, and stood up.

"I will drive you back," Madame Maury said, smiling.

"There's no need. It isn't far to walk. I can cut across your land, can't I?"

"Of course. It's a bit complicated until you reach the mountain, but after that you just follow the path around it till you get to the other side."

Madame Maury led Miranda into the garden and gave her careful directions that would bring her to the point where the two estates met.

"Don't forget to come and see me again."

"Even though I can't promise to help you?"

"Even though!" Madame Maury smiled.

Miranda set off down the slope. Much as she would enjoy seeing her hostess again, she did not feel she would be made welcome if Pierre put a high price on the land.

Yet the Maurys were business people and should expect such things to happen. Once the blue roses were grown she had no doubt about their commercial success. Neither had the Maurys: hence their determination to produce them. Besides, they were so wealthy that it would make little difference if the price was raised, whereas it would make a great deal of difference to her grandmother. And Pierre too, she admitted. Though she herself had no intention of accepting any financial gain from the sale, she knew he had no such inhibitions. And why should he have? He was not only a Chambray born but also a Chambray bred, which was more than could be said for *her*!

So immersed was she in thought that she reached the mountain path before she had expected it, and she paused and looked around her.

The grass here was thin and interspersed with rocky outcrops that made a random pattern on the sloping incline. A few stunted trees clung tenaciously to the sparse earth, their branches pointing downwards to where the waters of the *vallon* rushed precipitately along the narrow path that cut like a swathe of silver between one mountain and another. Yet they were not mountains in the strict sense of the word; for the most part their incline was so gradual that much of the land could be terraced and cultivated, and only here and there were sudden steep sections – almost vertical in appearance – which acted as nature's boundaries to mark one terrace from another.

She was curious to know what had caused these abrupt drops, for it was almost as if giant fingers had haphazardly scooped out sections of earth. It was probably due to erosion and might well mark the path of hidden mountain streams which had washed away the earth until only bedrock was left, leaving insufficient hold for trees. Without trees the land would become even sparser, and each succeeding winter's gales would erode more deeply into them until, over thousands of years, they had become the barren and dangerous fissures they now were.

Was it down one of these that the unknown Lucille had fallen to her death?

Or been pushed?

Miranda shivered. What had made her think such a thing? Pierre said he blamed Alain Maury for the tragedy, but surely he had meant a moral responsibility and not an actual physical one?

Once again she resumed walking. The path became narrower and more difficult, occasionally crumbling away beneath her feet so that she was forced to hold on to the stunted bushes that had taken the place of the grass. It was much harder going than she had envisaged, and the further she went the worse it became, the path almost disappearing so that several times she had to search for footholds on the rocks. The earth was porous and had an unpleasant way of slipping beneath her feet. Several times she felt herself sliding down towards the *vallon*, and only managed to stop herself by digging her hands hard into the ground. Not that any harm could come to her, she kept reassuring herself as she made laborious progress across the mountain. The incline was steep but not so precipitate that she would be unable to stop herself if she was unlucky enough to lose her footing. Gritting her teeth, she inched her way forward, wondering why Madame Maury had not warned her what to expect. She would certainly never come this way again.

Out of breath, she paused. Though it was well after midday the air here was cool. The sun did not penetrate far into this valley, and only the land above her lay basking in its rays. The sound of water was louder here, and though trees and bushes prevented her from seeing it she could not mistake its rush and gurgle. It was almost as if it had a life of its own and was talking to her. Annoyed at being so fanciful, she continued walking. If anything it became more difficult, for the ground was so slippery it was like walking on glass, and several times she was forced to sit down and inch forward on her buttocks, which did no good to her dress and even less to her temper.

Rubbing her hands, which were skinned and bleeding, she debated whether to retrace her steps or to continue, but deciding she had come more than halfway she resolutely pushed on. A large, smooth boulder loomed ahead, jutting out so far that it blocked her vision. It also blocked off the path she was trying to follow, and she realised she would either have to climb above it or below it. She gritted her teeth and decided to go below; at least if she fell she would not have so far to go.

Carefully she began to edge around the rock and, knowing she would not find any fingerhold on its surface, searched out for clumps of grass to give her more anchorage. The stream

68

seemed nearer from this point, and looking down she glimpsed swirling foam some fifty yards below. Would it be better to go right down to the bottom and hope to find a path beside it? She scanned the ground and decided to remain where she was.

Her decision was justified, for laboriously inching round the boulder she found herself back on the proper path. But a few more yards of scrabbling and she was once more facing an outcrop of rocks. It did not block her way as much as the first ones had done, and she was able to squeeze past them without difficulty. But nervous tension suddenly took hold of her and she sank down on one of the boulders and drew deep gulps of air, forcing herself to keep calm. She *must* be nearing the top of the mountain; it was impossible to think otherwise.

But fear rose up in her again and she felt sweat bead her forehead. Several strands of hair had escaped from her ponytail and lay in damp, dark gold tendrils on her forehead. With shaking hands she brushed them away from her face, then taking her handkerchief from her pocket, she tried to rub some of the dirt from her palms. But sharp pieces of grit were embedded in the skin and tears of pain made her stop. Putting her handkerchief away, she stood up and resumed walking.

She had only gone a few yards when falling stones made her stop again. Someone was ahead of her, hidden from sight by a twist in the path.

Even as she waited the steps came nearer. Instinctively she stiffened and, aware of it, chided herself for being silly. It was probably a shepherd looking for a sheep or goat that had strayed. Yet she had heard no animal bleating and she took a quick step forward, jerking back as a man came precipitately round the path and knocked into her.

"*Mon dieu!*" he exclaimed, and then stopped. "What on earth are *you* doing here?"

Miranda looked into Alain Maury's astonished gaze. "I'm on my way home."

"Across the *mountain*?"

"Obviously," she said sarcastically. "Or did you think I'd dropped down from heaven?"

"Not in that mood!" he answered, his mouth twitching slightly as he took in the angry sparkle of her eyes. "You look as angry as hell!"

"I might well have ended up there!" she retorted furiously. "Your mother must have been crazy to tell me to come back this way. If I'd lost my footing I could have broken my neck! As it is, I've ruined my hands." She flung them out. "Look at them!"

He stared at the red, bleeding skin, and instantly the sarcasm left his face. "Wait here," he ordered, and disappeared from sight almost as though he had melted into the very side of the mountain.

Only as she looked more closely did she notice a narrow aperture half hidden by an enormous bush, and cautiously she inched forward to peer inside. But the interior was black and gave nothing away, nor could she hear anything.

She stepped back and waited. A moment passed and then two. She drew a deep breath and was debating whether to move on when she heard footsteps again and almost at once he emerged from the cave holding a soaking wet handkerchief.

"There's a little spring back there," he explained. "I want to wash your hands."

"It can wait till I get home."

Ignoring her, he caught her wrists and with quick but surprisingly gentle movements dabbed at the skin, removing dried blood and several small flints. He worked intently, seemingly unaware of her eyes fixed on him, and she had a better opportunity to study him than at any time before.

Pierre was thirty-five, so that meant this man was thirty. He did not look it, for his face was unlined despite its gloomy expression, and there was a faun-like appearance to his physique. He looked up unexpectedly and she saw that his eyes were an unusual shade of brown. Like sherry that had been poured into a sunlit glass.

Annoyed at her fanciful thoughts, Miranda coloured and pulled her hands away from him.

"I don't think you'll find them so painful now," he said matter-of-factly.

Gingerly she flexed her fingers, wincing slightly. "They're much better. Thank you."

He regarded her, head on one side. "Am I to understand that my mother directed you to return home this way?"

"Yes."

"You must have misheard her – or else you missed the fork."

"What fork?"

"Where the paths meet." Seeing her blank look, the frown cleared from his forehead. "You come to it about a hundred yards after you start walking along the mountainside. A second path cuts across the main one. It descends for a few yards and –"

"I saw that," she interrupted, "but I didn't take it because I thought it led down to the *vallon*."

"It gives that impression, but in actual fact it twists up again and brings you out here." He inclined his head behind him.

"You mean I could have avoided all *that*?" She waved a hand along the path she had just come.

"Completely," he agreed. "The route you took is hardly walkable. Just a track for nimble-footed goats."

"And I'm no goat," she said ruefully. "No wonder I found it hard!"

"I must warn Mother to be more careful next time she gives directions. But I don't think she's ever come this way herself, so she doesn't know there are two paths." Once more he looked concerned. "It is most unfortunate you had to be a victim of her lack of knowledge."

"Not a victim," she said, mollified now that her hands were not stinging so badly, "but you should certainly tell her not to send anyone else this way without being more explicit."

71

"Strangers rarely take this short cut, and all the locals know it without having to be told."

His words, reminding her that this was not her home, also reminded her that she was not his friend, and with a polite movement she went to walk past him. But he turned and kept in step with her. "I'll see you safely back to the chateau."

"There's no need."

Ignoring her remark, he continued at her side, and though Miranda quickened her pace he appeared not to notice, merely lengthening his stride to match hers. Her breath came faster, but she set a quicker pace still, dismayed when she felt a sharp twinge in her side. For several yards she was able to overcome it, but she was finally forced to slow down, irritably aware that her companion showed no sign of discomfort, nor was he breathing any faster than normal.

"Rest a moment." His quiet order indicated his awareness of her pain.

In view of her flushed face and panting it would have been difficult to deny it, and she seated herself on a rock.

He remained standing in the centre of the path, his head thrown back, his shoulders stiff, so that again she was conscious of his tension.

"What were *you* doing on the path?" she asked.

"I often come here. Not many people do, and it gives me a chance of being alone to think." He hesitated. "I hope I will soon be hearing from your grandmother about the land?"

"Pierre will be calling you."

"I had hoped to avoid dealing with *him*."

"His interest is more than mine, Monsieur Maury. You can't expect him not to become involved."

"He hasn't bothered with the estate for years – why should he do so now?"

"Because you have made it valuable."

Alain Maury gave her a strange look. "I wonder if you realise the implication of your remark?"

"Of course I do. But it's no sin to be commercially minded. *You* are."

"I offered your grandmother a fair price for the land."

"Not all that fair if you're willing to double it!"

Colour warmed his tan. "I need the land and I need it at once if I'm not to miss next season. That's why I increased my price."

"I appreciate your urgency, *monsieur*, but you must also appreciate our fears."

"Fears of what?"

"Of regretting the sale once it's been made."

"Or of not holding out for an even higher price!"

"That too," she agreed.

"Everything has a value," he said tightly. "You would do well to remind Pierre of that."

"If the price Pierre asks is too high, you can refuse to buy."

"Is that what you want? There's no shortage of land in this part of Provence, Miss Dixon. On the coast maybe, but not here." He thrust his hands into the pockets of his slacks. The gesture pulled the blue material across his hips and she could see the taut line of his thighs. "It's only because this particular soil has the right mineral content that I want to buy it. But if *I* don't buy it no one else will!"

"Then my grandmother will be no worse off than she is now," Miranda said crisply.

"Nor will I."

"You want your perfume, don't you? Or do you have another formula up your sleeve?"

"Do you think they grow on trees?" he exploded. "It takes years to get successful ones! Making a new perfume isn't like making a dress. It takes hundreds of hours and dozens of people, and you can still end up with nothing!" His voice shook with fury. "For the first time in four years I've created a perfume I believe in — one that all women will want. But if I can't get the land to grow the roses, I might just as well throw

73

them away!"

There was so much anguish on his face that Miranda averted her head. She had never realised a perfume could mean so much to anyone that they could look as haunted as this dark-haired Frenchman was looking now. No wonder Madame Maury was so anxious for him.

"I hadn't realised the blue roses meant so much to you," she murmured as lightly as she could.

"You don't realise it even now," he said coldly. "To you and Pierre it's merely a question of money. But to me it's a question of –" He stopped, and when he continued his voice was without emotion. "If you continue a few yards further along the path, Miss Dixon, you will come out on to a lower lawn in front of the chateau."

Without another word he turned and walked away from her. Stones crumbled beneath his feet and a bush trembled as he passed it, then a bend in the path hid him from sight and she was left alone.

More moved than she cared to admit, Miranda continued on her way.

CHAPTER SIX

IT was one-fifteen when Miranda reached the chateau and, not even pausing to make herself tidy, ran into the dining room where her grandmother and Pierre were already seated.

"I'm sorry I'm late," she apologised, "but I took a short cut back from the village and got lost."

"We would have waited for you," the Comtesse said, "except that it was a soufflé – and they cannot be held up."

Acknowledging the truth of this, Miranda began to eat, glancing across at Pierre as she did so. She longed to know the outcome of his trip to Grasse but decided against asking him here. In one thing at least they were in accord: not to do or say anything that might make her grandmother excited or anxious.

Because of her suppressed anxiety lunch seemed to take longer than usual, and she marvelled that Pierre could mask his own feelings so successfully. Eventually the meal was over, the Comtesse retired to her room to rest and Pierre and Miranda were left to take their coffee on the lawn, in the shade of an orange tree.

"I had a most interesting morning in Grasse," he said without preamble. "I learned a lot about Alain's activities. Or perhaps I should say his *in*activities! The blue rose essence is the first perfume he's produced since Lucille's death. That's why he's so desperate to grow the flowers."

"I know. Madame Maury told me so this morning." Miranda quickly explained how they had met and what had been said.

"It all bears out what *I* heard," Pierre said triumphantly. "Alain's scared he's lost his creative talent. Perhaps he feels it's retribution for the way he behaved to Lucille."

"Why do you blame him for an accident?" Miranda asked

sharply. "It's the second time you've said it."

Thinking of her last encounter with Alain Maury – the way she had suddenly found him barring her path, his face inscrutable, the very air around him filled with tragedy – she could well believe he had something to do with the accident. But she could not believe he had encouraged his fiancée to kill herself.

"I'm sure her death was an accident," she said aloud.

"It was not," Pierre retorted. "Alain quarrelled with Lucille and told her he didn't want to marry her. That's why she committed suicide. If you don't believe me, read it for yourself in the back number of the local paper."

Miranda turned her head and looked at the bright sunshine dappling the lawn. All at once the grass seemed a more arid green and the sky a paler blue. Annoyed at her reactions, she tried to analyse them away. It was ridiculous to be partisan over someone she barely knew and did not like. Perhaps the British side of her character objected to having a man maligned in his absence.

"I don't know why you're telling me all this," she said. "Monsieur Maury's personal life has nothing to do with our selling him the land."

"It's got everything to do with it! You have all sorts of scruples about increasing the price, and I'm trying to make you see how foolish it is when you're dealing with someone like him!"

"I've no intention of dealing with him." Impatiently she jumped up. "*You* make the decision and talk it over with Grand'mère."

"She won't do anything without your approval. My own inclination is to let him sweat for a bit. Give him a few days and he'll increase his offer without being asked." There was a twinkle in the blue eyes. "In that way *I'll* be satisfied and so will your conscience – it's obviously bothering you to have to be businesslike towards a handsome Frenchman!"

Colour reddened her cheeks. "You're a handsome French-man, too, and I don't find it difficult to be businesslike with you!"

"We haven't talked business together," he retorted. "But thank you for the compliment anyway. I hope you mean it."

"You don't need *me* to flatter you. I imagine the girls must queue up to do so!"

"Only French ones," he admitted unblushingly, "and I've a penchant for the English." With one finger he delicately traced the line of her cheek, the tip of his nail coming to rest beside her lower lip. "What a stubborn mouth you have, my dear and distant cousin."

His head came lower, but with a deft movement she slipped away from him. "I must get on with my sketches – I'll see you at dinner."

"Are you running away?" he called after her retreating figure.

"Of course. I believe in being safe, not sorry!"

In the library, where she went in order to maintain the myth that she was going to work, Miranda found herself thinking of Madame Maury and her son. There was something mysterious and elusive about them. It came not only from the way they looked but from the very aura they exuded. Curiosity stirred within her, and though she hated herself for the thought, she knew she would go to the local newspaper offices and look through the back numbers to check on what Pierre had said.

From the distance the village clock struck four and, deter-mined to put all thoughts of the Maurys from her mind, she picked up a pencil and began to sketch. At first it was difficult to concentrate, but slowly her surroundings and all the people connected with it began to dissolve, leaving only blank sheets of paper to be filled in by swift sure lines that emanated from her fingertips like ectoplasm from a medium.

Not until the darkening of the sky made it necessary for her to get up and switch on the lamps did she realise she had been working for several hours, and she yawned and stretched with a feeling of pleasurable tiredness, then wandered back to the desk to look at what she had drawn.

The designs were good; looking at them with critical eyes there was no doubt of this. Indeed, they were the best she had yet done, with new ideas bursting from every sketch like buds from a branch.

There must be magic in the air, she thought, and flung her arms wide. "You're a magic chateau," she cried aloud. "My magic castle in Provence!"

"Talking to yourself, or may I join in?"

She spun round to see Pierre, a crystal decanter in one hand, two glasses in the other.

"A whisky for *l'heure bleue*," he added, pointing to the window which dusk was already turning into a sightless eye.

"I rarely get the blues," she said, declining the offer, "and whisky gives me hiccups!"

Setting down the decanter and glasses, he looked at the sketches on the desk. "May I?"

She nodded, and he bent over the loose leaves of paper. One by one he lifted them up and looked at them; casually at first but gradually becoming more intent.

"They're sensational," he said finally. "Original without being gimmicky."

"They're not bad," she agreed.

"Are they for your new Collection?"

"Hopefully. But I can't afford to make them all up. I'll have to choose a dozen of the best."

"They are all excellent."

"They need a bit more working on," she said, deciding to quench the flow of compliments.

"Agreed." He riffled through the pile and picked out a sketch of a suit and an evening dress. "These don't fit in with your general theme. They're too fussy. Best take out the pleats and cut down on the number of buttons, and they'll do fine."

She was astonished. "Don't tell me *you're* a designer too?"

"I am interested in it," he said modestly. "Some of my girl-friends are models!"

"Girl-*friends*?" she quizzed.

"All my ex-mistresses are my friends!"

She laughed and perched on the edge of the chair. "It *will* be hard having to choose twelve from this lot."

"Can't you find a backer?"

"I don't want one. I want to be free to design what *I* like."

"Couldn't you be?"

"He who pays the piper calls the tune," Miranda said drily.

"*I* know someone who wouldn't. Someone who'd let you play any tune you liked."

"Pull the other one!" she retorted.

"I'm not joking." He poured himself a whisky and drank it at a gulp. "Have you heard of Christi's?"

"Of course. It was a top fashion house till Jacques Christi died. I've not heard about them since."

"They're still ticking over — just. Two new designers were brought in to take Christi's place, but neither of them were good enough. The last one was fired a month ago and they're looking for a replacement. I think you would do admirably."

"Now I *know* you're joking!"

"Not at all." Pierre poured another drink. "Christi's is backed by Tissus Maurice — one of the biggest textile compan-ies in France — and Monsieur Maurice is determined to keep Christi's going as an outlet for his fabrics. A successful couturier makes an excellent shop window for the fashion world to look at."

"No fashion house can keep going without a decent collec-tion," Miranda said.

"That's why I want your sketches. Our company handles his advertising, so I know him fairly well."

"You're wasting your time. He'll want an established name for Christi's."

"They brought in two top names and failed with them both! That's why I'm sure it's worth a try. If Maurice likes your work, he won't be put off because you haven't got a big name." Pierre strode over and caught her shoulders. "Where's your faith in yourself? I thought you were convinced you were going to the top?"

"I am," she said staunchly, "but I expect to do it in my own way."

"Wouldn't you accept an offer from Tissus Maurice?"

"Of course I would. It's the sort of thing you dream about."

"Then dream a bit longer. I hope I can make it come true." He bent his head and swiftly kissed her lips.

From the loose way he held her she knew he did not mean to do more, but as he felt the touch of her mouth his grip tightened and he kissed her again, more slowly and deeply. Miranda tried to resist him, but he was too expert, his touch too skilful, and without being able to stop herself, she was aroused.

"Well, well," he murmured, drawing away from her. "Tante Emilie's hopes might not be so far-fetched after all!"

"Don't bank on it!"

He gave a soft laugh and, returning to the desk, picked up her sketches and went to the door. "I'll try and see Maurice tomorrow."

"But you've only just arrived here. Grand'mère will be disappointed if you leave so soon."

"I won't be leaving. Maurice has a house at Cap d'Antibes. He flies down most weekends. With luck he should be there tomorrow."

She caught her breath. "You make it sound so easy."

"Everything's easy if you know the right people!"

He went out, and after turning off the lamps, Miranda did the same.

As she changed for dinner into a black silk pleated dress that emphasised her creamy skin, she thought of what Pierre was going to do. Tissus Maurice was world-renowned, and to be promoted by them could lead to undreamed-of success. Yet despite this, two people had already failed. It was a sobering thought and she forced herself to consider the dangers that such backing could hold for her.

Her talent might be enough to excite the buyers in London, but was it enough to interest a world-wide market controlled by hard-faced men and women who dictated the tune to which the *couture* carousel turned? It was a frightening thought and her heart hammered against her ribs. It was not too late to tell Pierre she did not want him to show her sketches to anyone. She could take them back and continue with her own plans in her own time. The thought was tempting – as playing safe always was – but there was not a spark of red in her hair for nothing, and dismissing safety, she decided to leave things as they were and let fate take over.

A mild indisposition sent the Comtesse early to bed that night, and Pierre suggested taking Miranda to Cannes.

"We can be there by nine and try our luck at the tables."

"The best way of trying my luck is to keep *away* from the tables!"

He chuckled. "Then just come and keep me company."

"I'm too tired." She looked at him with some curiosity. "I'm sure you have other friends in Cannes more than willing to amuse you."

"Dozens," he agreed. "But none as nice as you." He sauntered across to her, hands in the pockets of his trousers. His stance reminded her of Alain Maury, who was so different in temperament and outlook. But then tragedy had left its mark on him, and she wondered what he had been like before the death of the unknown Lucille.

"What are you thinking about?" Pierre asked.

She shrugged, unwilling to let him know her thoughts.

"Are you sure you won't come to Cannes?"

81

"Positive. But don't let me stop *you* from going."

He looked apologetic. "Even a couple of days in the country give me the creeps."

"You're obviously no nature-lover!"

"Are you?"

"I love it *here*," she admitted.

"Because you know it's only for a holiday. You'd hate it if it were permanent."

"I'm not sure. I might decide to give up work and settle for marriage and a cottage in the country!"

"Your talent would never let you rest. You've a seeing eye and you'll only be happy when you're using it."

"You make me sound like a guide dog!"

He grinned. "That's what you are. The seeing eye of fashion; leading those who have no vision themselves!"

It was an ingenious compliment and impulsively she reached up to kiss his cheek. But he was too quick for her and turned his head so that their lips met.

Almost at the same moment she glimpsed a movement by the curtain and quickly drew back. But no one came in through the window and she decided it had only been a breeze stirring the material.

"Go to Cannes for your gamble," she smiled. "I'll come and see you off."

Together they went to the front door where his low-slung sports car gleamed in the moonlight.

"What a vicious-looking thing it is," Miranda remarked.

"Like its owner?"

"You said it, not me!"

She watched as he vaulted into the front seat, switched on the ignition and drove off in a burst of exhaust fumes. Pulling a face at the noise and smell, she turned to go inside, and then changed her mind and went down the steps and across the lawn.

Like a tall dark shadow she moved over the grass, long skirts

82

falling gracefully around her, long thick hair framing a face which the moonlight blanched of all colour. The landscape was colourless too, with black trees silhouetted against the sky and black shadows lying jagged on the ground. A breeze stirred the foliage near at hand and a night animal – disturbed in its prowl for food – scampered away at her approach.

Behind her loomed the house, seeming twice as large in the dark as it did in the daylight, while in front of her the undulating hills appeared steeper, reminding her of the mountain and the sharp descent to the *vallon*. She craned her neck, but a bank of trees hid the mountain from sight. Yet its presence pervaded the atmosphere, and though she knew it was only imagination she was sure she could hear the ice-cold waters rushing on their way to nowhere. A bird called in a tree, a high plaintive sound that startled her, and she picked up her skirts and sped back across the grass.

Straight into the smothering hold of a tall, black figure.

She gave a muffled scream, the sound dying away as the grip relaxed and a quiet voice said : "I didn't mean to startle you."

Astonished, she saw it was Alain Maury. "What are *you* doing here?"

"I came to apologise. I was unnecessarily rude to you this morning."

"So it *was* you on the terrace !" she said involuntarily.

"Yes. You seemed busy and I – I didn't want to intrude."

"You wouldn't have been. I was only turning down Pierre's offer to go to Cannes."

"Are your turn-downs always so demonstrative?"

"What's a kiss?" she shrugged.

"Something that shouldn't be given lightly."

"You're old-fashioned, *monsieur*." She set off across the lawn towards the terrace.

He kept in step beside her. "I'm sorry if I have annoyed you. I didn't mean to."

"You always annoy me."

83

"We must have an incompatibility of spirit!" He spoke insouciantly, yet there was nothing uncaring about the look on his face; lit by a sudden shaft of moonlight it appeared bitter and haunted. "I had hoped we might be kindred spirits, Miss Dixon. That *your* ambition would help you to understand *mine.*"

"I understand you very well. But it doesn't mean we're kindred spirits!"

They entered the drawing-room and he carefully latched the window before coming to stand by the mantelpiece. He was elegantly dressed in black: suede shoes, barathea trousers and black cashmere sweater. It made him look very lean and slight, which was surprising, for he topped her by several inches.

"I hope the Comtesse is well?" he asked.

"She has gone to bed. She was feeling tired."

"Not ill, I hope?"

"Certainly not." Miranda spoke sharply and the man seemed taken aback.

"I do not wish the Comtesse any harm. It was a genuine enquiry."

Miranda blushed. "I'm sorry. I'm sure it was."

"I have already told you I didn't come to see your grandmother," he continued. "I came to see you to –"

"Apologise for being rude to me," she reminded him.

"And also came to bring you these." He held out his hand and she saw four tubes of gouache.

"How did you know I wanted them?"

"Colette told me. I happened to have some at the laboratory and I thought they might tide you over till you get some more."

The thoughtfulness of the gesture left her speechless. More so because it was unexpected. Contrition warred with the antagonism she felt towards him, and murmuring her thanks, he took the tubes and put them on the table.

"Would you care for a drink, *monsieur*?"

84

"A brandy would be welcome." He accepted it from her. "Aren't you going to join me?"

"I don't like the taste. The last time I had any it was to stop me from fainting!"

"What a waste of brandy! It can only be appreciated when one has total control of oneself."

"Then you should be able to drink it all the time!"

Deliberately he studied her. "You have a strange conception of my character. Contrary to your assumption, I frequently lose my control. You should talk to my staff!"

He twirled the glass in his fingers. They were long and slender, she noted, yet very strong. He was now looking at the brandy with the same intensity he had deployed on her. It was the sort of look often seen on young children. Not that there was anything childlike in his expression as he lifted his eyes to hers.

"Your hair is the same colour as the brandy, Miss Dixon."

"It's lighter."

"Not at night." He held the goblet high so that the light from the chandelier glowed through the liquid. "It's exactly this colour," he repeated. "But during the day it is the colour of honey."

The compliment embarrassed her and she tried to make a joke of it. "Brandy and honey. Are your comparisons always centred round food and drink?"

"I'm a Frenchman!"

She smiled and sat down on the settee. For the first time she saw virtue in her grandmother's incessant sewing; at least it kept one's hands occupied. Clasping hers together, she searched vainly for something to say.

However, the silence did not disconcert her visitor and he sat down opposite her and crossed one leg over the other, his back rigid, his head high.

"Don't you ever relax?" she burst out.

"I'm doing so now."

"You're as stiff as a poker!"

Her words made him consider his position, and he moved his shoulders and uncrossed his legs. "Is that better?"

"Not much."

"I don't find it easy to relax," he confessed so apologetically that she laughed.

"You can say that again. You give the impression of a fire-cracker ready to go off at any minute."

"That is some kind of firework, is it not?"

She nodded. "It's a special kind that jumps all over the place and keeps exploding."

"I had not realised you thought me so dangerous!"

He chuckled, looking so much younger that she was amazed. Even his features changed when he smiled, his mouth softening into a pleasing curve, his eyes seeming larger when no longer marked by scowling brows.

"You should smile more often, *monsieur*. It makes you look human."

"To be human is to be vulnerable." The smile left his face abruptly. "And to be vulnerable is to leave oneself open to hurt."

"You can't go through life closed up like a clam! You'll miss out on so many other emotions if you do."

"I have no wish for emotion. It robs a man of strength."

"It can *give* you strength. Think of all the wonderful things people have done when they were emotionally inspired. The paintings and music that have been created; the books that have been written and –"

"Not with emotion," Alain Maury said vehemently. "With passion of mind, perhaps, but not with emotion."

"What's the difference between the two?"

"One is mental and of the spirit; the other is earthly and of the flesh."

"You sound like a tub-thumping Puritan! What's *wrong* with earthly love? It makes the world go round!"

"You can do better than *that* trite comment."

"Because you had an unhappy love affair it doesn't give you the right to mock everyone else." She stopped abruptly, her embarrassment increasing as she saw the lines of bitterness on his face. "I'm sorry, *monsieur*. I had no right to say that."

"You listen to gossip," he shrugged. "I am not surprised. Rural communities thrive on having a villain in their midst."

"Don't you mind?"

He shook his head. "People believe what they want to. I have no intention of trying to alter their opinions. Lucille is dead and nothing will bring her back. The episode is over."

Miranda was unable to credit his prosaic tones. It was as if he were talking about a stranger and not a girl he had loved. "You make it sound as if she never existed."

"She didn't."

"What do you mean?"

"Forget it. Let us talk about something else."

"You're a hard man, Monsieur Maury."

"I am a realist."

The words reminded her of Pierre, though she could see no similarity between the two men. Pierre was a realist, but he was also warm and spontaneous, whereas this man was cold and calculating.

"I don't think we have anything more to talk about, *monsieur*. It is late and I –"

"We can talk about the blue rose," he said, "and the land I am anxious to buy."

"Is that all you care about? Land for your flowers."

"My blue roses are beautiful. They deserve to bloom."

"No wonder you've no time for emotion," she retorted. "You give it all to your flowers!"

"Do I?" With a swiftness she had not anticipated he was on his feet and gripping her by the shoulders. "Do I?" he said again, and pulled her into his arms. There was no tenderness in his touch, no warmth to his kiss, just a deep, raw passion that

87

demanded a response. And how skilfully he drew one from her! Detached and remote he might look, but there was nothing detached about the pressure of his mouth which, feeling hers move beneath his, became insistent and searching. Held close in his arms, Miranda felt trapped by steely muscles. There was not an ounce of superfluous fat on him. It was as if his driving energy burned him up, giving him a tense vulnerability that added to the complexity of his character.

Not that there was anything complex in his actions, for he was the all-conquering male asserting his strength, arousing her ardour by the depth of his own. What had begun as a kiss of fury was now one of passion, and unable to stop herself, her arms came round his neck to draw him closer.

They drew apart simultaneously and stared at each other, hazel eyes shining, brown ones brooding. Though she was not sure what she had expected from him, she had not anticipated the furious way he put the distance of the room between them. The gesture was more hurtful than any words could have been, and she was dismayed by the hurt she felt. For a brief moment she had believed herself mentally close to this man, and his abrupt withdrawal showed her all too clearly that the affinity had not been mutual.

"I shouldn't have done that," he muttered.

"Forget it." She marvelled that her voice could be so unconcerned. "We're in the twentieth century."

"Ah yes. The permissive society."

"That's an old-fashioned phrase these days, *monsieur*. But then you *are* old-fashioned. It accounts for you trying to use sex to win an argument!"

The remark struck home and he reddened, looking more saturnine than ever. "You weren't above using it yourself, *mademoiselle*. You deliberately provoked me."

It was impossible for her to disagree, and she was wondering whether to ignore the remark or make some sarcastic rejoinder when she heard voices in the hall.

She hurried across and opened the door. Colette Dinard stood there, elegant in long black satin skirt and jacket, pink crêpe blouse giving a warm sheen to her skin. Her short hair, sleek as ever, curved into the nape of her neck, showing off the well-shaped head and making her look like an elegantly dressed boy, or one of that strange breed of bizarre young women who had flourished in Germany between the two world wars. She was not at all the sort of person Miranda would have imagined capable of holding Alain Maury's attention, though perhaps this was because in picturing Lucille, the very name itself conjured up someone feminine and childlike, neither of which adjectives applied to the ice-cool Miss Dinard.

"Forgive me coming here like this," the French girl said, "but Alain promised to be back in half an hour and I was worried."

Failing to discern any worry in the hard eyes, Miranda was convinced that curiosity alone had brought Colette here. Was she so worried about holding Alain Maury's attentions that she had to follow him to the chateau?

"Sorry, Colette, but it took me longer to get here than I had anticipated." The man came into the conversation for the first time, sounding faintly amused, as though he saw the truth behind her subterfuge. "You could have saved yourself a journey by telephoning."

"I couldn't get through. You know what village telephones are like."

"Now that you're here, I hope you will stay for a drink?" An imp of mischief prompted Miranda to play the *grande dame*. It would certainly be different from the ingenue she had appeared to be when she had met the French girl in the village this morning!

"There's no need to disturb yourself on our behalf," Alain said quickly.

"I'd love a drink," Colette Dinard overrode him, and stepped into the salon, looking around her with a curiosity she made no attempt to hide.

As she sipped a Grand Marnier she wandered around, picking up and putting down various objets d'art, almost as though she was an auctioneer coming to value the contents of the house. Miranda felt her shackles rise and slipped her thumbs beneath the wide jewelled belt that clasped her narrow waist.

"Haven't you seen the chateau before, Miss Dinard?" she enquired.

"Only from the outside, and even then not until Alain told me of his intention to buy the land."

"My *hope* to buy it," he amended. "So far the offer has not been accepted."

"Surely it will be?" Colette stared openly at Miranda. "The land's just being wasted!"

"My grandmother cannot make up her mind," Miranda explained, "and she is going to let Pierre decide."

Colette laughed and looked at Alain. "Then you've nothing to worry about. Pierre's a business man down to his fingertips."

From the remark, Miranda guessed the girl knew Pierre, and she wondered why he had not told her so this evening. She would ask him about her tomorrow. She was curious to know Colette's background and her relationship to the man whom she treated so proprietorially.

"We must be going, Alain." Colette set down her glass and gave Miranda an empty smile. "Thank you so much for the drink, and please give my compliments to the Comtesse."

"She will be sorry not to have met you." Miranda played the game of formality to its close.

"Another time perhaps," red-tipped fingers rested on Alain's black-clad arm. "I brought the car with me, *chéri.* I didn't think you'd want to walk back as well."

"That was thoughtful of you." He glanced at Miranda. "Thank you for your hospitality, *mademoiselle.* I hope we will meet again soon."

"I see no need for it," Miranda replied coldly. "I expect you'll be hearing from Pierre."

Her answer had the desired effect, for again colour ran up into Alain Maury's face. Silently he went out of the chateau and took the passenger seat of Colette's low-slung Italian car. It purred away as softly as a departing panther, and not until its tail lights disappeared round a curve in the drive did she enter the hall.

What a strange ending to a strange day! So many incidents flashed through her mind that it was like looking at a kaleidoscope where everything formed a jumble and no cohesive pattern emerged: Pierre's determination to get the highest price for the land; her own ambivalence towards it sale due to her longing to live here and her equally strong urge to build a career for herself; Madame Maury's devotion to her son and her son's devotion to the blue rose. And above all, this last meeting with Alain Maury.

How strangely he had spoken of his fiancée. What had he meant when he said the girl had never existed? And how could you love someone who did not exist?

There was no answer to any of these questions, though the questions themselves gave credence to the gossip which Pierre had said was rife about Alain's relationship with Lucille. If the girl had never existed for him, it was easy to infer that he had not loved her. Was it this knowledge that had sent her plunging to her death? Somehow Miranda could no longer believe the fall had been an accident.

Disturbed by her thoughts, she tried to rationalise them. No normal girl would end her life because of a broken engagement. Nor would any man goad his fiancée into killing herself in order to get rid of her. What had really happened between them? She refused to believe he had become engaged to satisfy his mother's desire to see him married. He had far too much character to be persuaded into doing such a thing. Could it have been a simple change of heart – the realisation that he did not want to give up his freedom after all? And could Lucille – heartbroken – have committed suicide because of it?

Miranda pushed her hair away from her head. Would *she* commit suicide if she were jilted by the man she loved? Would any girl – other than an unstable one – do so in this day and age? Remembering Pierre's injunction that she read Lucille's letter and judge for herself, she decided to do exactly as he had suggested.

"I'm turning into a gossipmonger," she thought, and said the words aloud, hoping that by doing so she would destroy their credibility. But curiosity remained with her. Nothing gave a man a more glamorous image than to be the centre of a mystery, and the only way to stop thinking of him was to find out the whole truth about him.

Destroy the myth, and the man was destroyed with it.

Tomorrow she would go to Nice and read the newspapers.

CHAPTER SEVEN

SLEEP was a long time coming to Miranda that night, for she kept thinking of the blue rose and what it meant to Alain Maury. When she finally did sleep he came into her dreams in a far more disturbing way; running with her across a field ablaze with blue flowers and then twirling her round in his arms until they fell to the ground breathless, and she sank into the soft earth beneath the pressure of his body.

She awoke so suddenly that the dream was still with her, and she moved her legs, surprised to find she was lying on a mattress and not on flowers. Quickly she sat up, gaining comfort from the stolid furniture and the daylight seeping in through the half-closed shutters. Clouds unexpectedly marched across the sky and the air was chilly and damp, as though it was going to rain.

Rain it did, an hour later when she was having breakfast in the dining room, and she was debating whether to continue with her sketches when Pierre came in, heavy-eyed and irritable.

"No luck at the tables," she ventured.

"Positively bad luck," he said glumly.

"You shouldn't gamble if you can't afford it," she said heartlessly.

"There's no excitement gambling with what you *can* afford."

"Can't you find more rewarding excitement?"

"I'm looking," he smiled, some of his good humour returning as he poured some coffee and straddled the chair beside her. "If Maurice likes your designs, I intend to swing myself a job at Christi's."

"I can't see you selling clothes!"

"I was thinking of the business side. Someone has to keep putting the name of the company in front of the public. Publicity doesn't happen by itself. Once you're there I can—"

"Let's wait till it happens."

"That shouldn't be long," he said. "I spoke to Maurice last night and we're seeing him this evening!"

With shaking hands Miranda set down her cup. "I don't think I'll go with you."

"Nonsense. Maurice isn't just backing a talent. He's backing the person too. He made that very clear when I spoke to him. He's had enough of airy-fairy dress designers and wants to make sure that choice number three has both feet on the ground."

"I wish I had some press cuttings with me."

"Forget it. Just see him tonight and sell *yourself*."

She sighed. "It isn't just a question of a backer investing in a dress designer. It's Christi's cloak being put on the shoulders of an unknown."

"A cloak without someone inside it is just a shroud," Pierre reminded her. "At the moment the House of Christi is a corpse. I'm putting *you* forward as the one person who can breathe life into it."

"I wish you could have chosen a less depressing simile!"

"I was fitting it to your mood of self-depreciation!" He stood up. "We'll have dinner in Antibes tonight and get to Maurice around nine. Right now I'm off to Nice. Care to come with me?"

"I'd love to."

Not until she accepted the offer did she realise how anxious she was to learn the full story of Lucille's death, and though she despised her curiosity she was too intelligent to fight it.

"I was fitting it to your mood of self-depreciation!" The winding road down to the coast was mercifully free of coaches which, Pierre informed her, were the bane of one's life during the summer months. A few miles above Cannes they branched

94

off to take the motorway, though it ended when they were still some distance from the city and they had to continue on a tortuously narrow and congested road into the town itself.

"If you want to go anywhere special," Pierre said, "I'll drop you off."

Reluctant to tell him what she was going to do, she murmured that she only wanted to do some window-shopping, and he left her outside the Galeries Lafayette, arranging to meet her a couple of hours later at the Café Royal on the Promenade des Anglais.

As soon as he had driven off, Miranda made her way to the offices of *Nice Matin*.

Like most newspaper buildings this one was busy and casual, and her request to look at old editions met with such disinterest that she almost gave up the attempt. But eventually she found herself in a dingy room facing a mound of yellowing papers.

"Don't get them out of order," an old man adjured her, "and don't tear bits out!"

Promising not to do so, she leafed through the pages. It was disconcerting how guilty she felt, almost as though she were prying into secrets and not something which was common knowledge and available for anyone to see if they wished.

The search was laborious, made more difficult by not knowing exactly what she was looking for, and she had almost given up hope of finding what she wanted when the name "Bayronne" stared up at her.

Quickly she began to read. It was a short account of the discovery of the body of Lucille Dufy who had fallen to her death while out walking. "Mountain claims second victim in five years," the article ran, and went on to state that there had been several accidents at this particular spot, which was made more dangerous in winter and spring by torrential rainfall.

There was also a photograph of Lucille, and for a long moment Miranda stared at it, surprised by the complexity of emotions that went through her as she saw the plaintive-looking face with its soulful eyes and dark hair. It was a face made for tragedy, as though the camera lens had caught the future of this beautiful yet haunted-looking girl.

Sombrely Miranda picked up the next edition of the paper and learned that Alain Maury had been interrogated for several hours by an inspector sent from Paris. For the first time mention was made of a letter found in Lucille's coat, though the contents were not disclosed, and she had to thumb through several more weeks' papers before blazing headlines drew her attention to what the writer of the article called "The tragedy of Lucille Dufy."

For an instant Miranda closed her eyes, overcome by revulsion at what she was doing, but she had progressed too far to stop now, and she opened her eyes and began to read.

The sordid ugliness of the story emerged from the yellowing pages with an evil life of their own. It was a story that must have happened many times before, and Miranda was furious for not having guessed it. Yet its very obviousness had prevented her from doing so; as if the obvious could never figure in Alain Maury's life.

Lucille had been expecting Alain's child when she died.

The knowledge filled Miranda with unexpected repugnance. She was no prissy Victorian Miss who did not know the facts of life. Why was she surprised that Lucille and Alain had anticipated their marriage? Was it because she could not imagine him being overcome by passion? Remembering the way he had kissed her last night she knew this was untrue.

Turning back to the paper, she found the copy of Lucille's letter to Alain. Here at last was what she had had to see. With fast beating heart she began to read, forcing herself to go slowly and not misinterpret. But there was no chance of doing that. Clearly and concisely the letter indicted him, making him as guilty of Lucille's death as if he had actually pushed her over the mountain ledge.

How easy it was to see the turmoil in the girl's mind when, having told him she was expecting his child, he had callously said he did not want to marry her. A person of a hardier temperament might not have been so overcome, but to a girl who, according to the newspaper accounts, had led a sheltered life in a convent until she was eighteen, and then come to live with her godmother, Adrienne Maury, it must have seemed like the end of the world.

Again Miranda read the letter. It was obvious that Alain had never loved his fiancée, as it was obvious that she could not live if he no longer wanted to marry her.

"When you love someone with all your heart, you don't count the cost of what you do or worry about the future. I gave myself completely because it was the only way I could show my love, and even your fury when you learned I was pregnant hasn't made me regret what I did. I always feel in my heart that I wasn't the right person for you.

"Knowing the man you are, I know you'll be sorry for all the things you said to me, and I'd like you to know that I'm not angry. I'm not miserable either. The happiness I've had has been enough for me. My only sorrow is that the child won't —"

Here the letter ended, and Miranda wondered what emotions had made it impossible for the girl to go on. How could Alain have behaved so despicably? If he had been so unsure about Lucille that she had guessed it herself, how could he have so callously seduced her? For that was what he had done. Lucille had not been a sophisticated woman, but a trusting innocent who had loved him too much to turn him away.

"Have you found what you wanted, mademoiselle?" The old man had come back into the room, and startled, Miranda turned to look at him.

"Yes, thank you. I was just going."

He looked at her curiously. "You are pale. Can I get you some water?"

"No, thank you, *monsieur*. I'm meeting a friend at the Café Royal and I'll have a drink there."

Leaving him to his yellowed press cuttings, she set off briskly for the Promenade des Anglais.

The day had brightened considerably, but as far as she was concerned the heavens were still weeping, as she was weeping inside for an unknown girl whose tragedy had touched her so deeply. With the stench of guilt in his nostrils, it was not surprising that Alain Maury had been afraid he had lost the ability to create any more perfume. She quickened her pace, as though by so doing she could leave all thoughts of him behind. But his ghost marched in step with her and she started to run along the pavement, only stopping as she knocked full tilt into the grey-suited figure of a man rounding a corner. The breath was knocked from her body, and she was only saved from falling by a pair of steadying hands.

"Do you always make it a habit to run like a wild thing?" a quiet voice asked, and Miranda gasped and found herself looking into the brown eyes of the man from whose very thought she had been trying to escape.

"You!" she said. "What are you doing here?"

"We seem to have had this conversation before, too," he said whimsically, and took his hands away from her. "I had a meeting with my lawyer and I'm on my way home. And you, Miss Dixon?"

"I'm going to the Café Royal."

"They do excellent coffee. Will you permit me to share a cup with you?"

Not knowing how to refuse, she nodded and walked in silence beside him.

The café was one of the largest along the promenade, with numerous tables protected from the sunlight by blue and white umbrellas. With the quiet ease which Miranda was beginning to associate with him, Alain found a vacant table, ordered coffee and was almost immediately served.

"Have you been shopping in Nice?" he asked conversationally.

She shrugged. What she had learned about him was still too raw in her mind for her to talk to him with ease, and she made a pretence of being absorbed in choosing a cake she did not want from the trolley which a waiter had wheeled to a stop in front of her.

"I recommend the *framboise*," Alain Maury said, and picking up a plate and fork, took one for himself.

"I'll just stick to coffee," Miranda said, knowing she could not swallow anything.

"Aren't you well?" he asked. "When you knocked into me you looked as though you were being pursued by devils."

Again she did not answer, and after giving her a thoughtful look he fixed his attention to the passing parade. A motley crowd presented itself before him. Elegantly dressed couples taking the air at their ease; elderly women with frizzy dyed hair and frizzy-hued poodles high-stepping past on their way to nowhere, and a spattering of boys and girls, arms entwined and buttocks swinging in tight-fitting jeans.

"I'm sorry Colette arrived when she did last night," he said unexpectedly. "Our conversation was just becoming interesting."

"We had already talked too much!"

"I don't agree with you." Imps of mischief danced in his warm brown eyes. "You have an independent mind and I would like to explore it."

"Lots of women have independent minds."

"But they are often so aggressive with it." The twinkle grew more pronounced. "*You* have retained your femininity."

"Not enough to arouse your chivalry, *monsieur*. You still tried to race me for a taxi."

"*Allons!* Must you always go back to that?"

"I don't forget easily."

A shadow crossed his face, and she wondered whether he was aware of her meaning. Yet he could not be, for he had no idea where she had been.

"Did you always want to be a dress designer?" His change of subject disconcerted her, and she nodded. "I'd like to see your work."

"You wouldn't like it." She hesitated. "I designed my emerald suit."

"Ah." He smiled. "Are all your clothes so bright and astringent?"

"I hate labels, *monsieur*."

"But you have labelled *me* in your mind." He rested his elbows on the table and she noticed how well shaped his hands were. "To you, I am the ungallant Frenchman who insulted your womanhood by wanting your taxi, and then made matters worse by insulting your taste in clothes!"

Against her will she smiled, and seeing it he smiled back. As always it transformed his face, his aloofness giving way to unexpected sensuality. No man had the right to look so devastatingly handsome, she thought crossly, and pushed her chair further away from the table. She knew he was flirting with her and she wondered how she would have reacted under normal circumstances. But the circumstances could never be normal between them. No matter how hard she tried, his past would always form an immovable barrier.

"Please don't let me delay you," she said in her coldest voice.

"Why are you so keen to dismiss me? We're neighbours, Miss Dixon. Do you not have a neighbourly interest in me?"

Before she could reply a boy stopped at their table. "You are the English lady who was at the *Nice Matin* office?" he enquired.

"Y-yes," she stammered.

"Monsieur Rocchia found this in one of the back copies of the paper."

100

He held out a blue glove which she recognised as her own, and she hurriedly fumbled in her bag for a franc, all the time aware of Alain Maury sitting beside her as though carved of stone. The boy thanked her and moved away, and only then did the man speak, his voice full of contempt.

"So that's why you came to Nice! You had to satisfy your curiosity." He leaned forward and gripped her arm. "You should have asked *me*, Miss Dixon. I'd have told you what you wanted to know."

"I *couldn't* ask you," she said tightly. "And I – I didn't want to listen to other people's gossip."

"That at least is commendable. The written word, however cruel, is not as cruel as people's tongues." He folded his arms across his chest. The colour had not yet returned to his face, and despite its tan it held a tinge of greyness. "I take it you're now satisfied?"

"At least I know what happened."

"Do *you* despise me too?"

"I try not to judge other people's behaviour, *monsieur*."

"An excellent sentiment," he taunted, "but hardly true. I can see from your expression that you too have judged me and found me wanting. You needn't be ashamed of it. You are in excellent company. Like all the other good people of Bayronne, you have the same narrow point of view."

"Is it narrow to have compassion?" she burst out. "Are you so heartless that you don't regret what you did?"

He stood up abruptly, his chair crashing to the ground behind him. Several people stared in their direction and he bent and picked it up. "You are right, Miss Dixon, we've already talked too much." He placed a ten-franc note under his saucer and turned to go.

As he did so he saw Pierre Chambray approaching, and his face grew even paler.

"Hallo, Alain," Pierre said easily. "I'm not interrupting you both, am I?"

"Since when would that have stopped you?" Alain asked harshly.

Colour darkened Pierre's cheeks. "Still the same Alain," he smiled.

"Did you expect me to change?"

"I never expect the impossible!" Pierre reached out for a chair from another table. "Don't let me drive you away."

"You haven't," Alain said, and nodding in Miranda's direction, threaded his way through the tables and out of sight.

His going left a vacuum which Pierre tried to fill with chatter, but she did not hear a word he said, and was glad when she finally found herself in his car driving back to Bayronne.

"What were you and Alain arguing about?" Pierre asked suddenly. "He looked in a flaming temper."

She stared steadfastly through the window, wondering why the sea should look grey when she knew it was turquoise blue. "I went to the office of *Nice Matin* and read about Lucille. He found out."

"So that was it! Still, it's as well he knows you're wise to him. It'll stop him playing on your sympathy to get the land."

"I've already told him Grand'mère's leaving the decision to you."

"Alain's a great believer in the power of his persuasion!"

"He must be," Miranda said tremulously, and thought of Lucille, who had succumbed to it and been destroyed by it.

"Do you think he *was* to blame for her death?" she asked suddenly.

"Don't you know the answer without my telling you?"

"I suppose so," she sighed, "but I can't believe it. If he didn't love her, why did he pretend?"

"To satisfy his mother."

"It was so cruel."

"He *is* cruel." Pierre caught her hand. "Stop thinking about a past that isn't yours. Think of the future instead. *Our* future."

His exuberance lapped at her depression, and though it did not wash it way completely, it smoothed off the sharp edges so that only sadness remained with her during the long drive back to the chateau.

Miranda's nervousness at meeting Monsieur Maurice forced Alain Maury from her mind. It was all very well for Pierre to talk blithely of her becoming chief designer at Christi's, but was she ready for such a major position?

And equally important — would it be offered to her? Would her confidence be destroyed if Maurice turned her down? After all, he had already shown his fallibility by choosing two non-starters!

Miranda fought against the depression by wearing her prettiest dress: a long skirt and blouse in hand-painted chiffon with ruffles at her throat and wrists. She piled her hair on top of her head, surprised at how defenceless her neck looked when it was bare, as though it could be snapped by a single blow from a lean dark hand . . .

Quickly she pushed the thought away and ran downstairs.

"You look like a flower," her grandmother said as she entered the drawing-room.

"Like the entire flower-bed!" Pierre corrected, and repeated his compliment as they drove down to Antibes. "You look exceptionally lovely tonight. I feel in my bones that things are going to work out well."

"Don't bank on it, Pierre. Feelings can be wrong."

He shook his head, then concentrated on the road. The bends appeared more tortuous at night, but with less traffic about they made good time, and soon the lights of Antibes were strung out before them like diamonds round the throat of a dark beauty.

Unlike Cannes, which was busy even late at night, Antibes closed down at eight, and the Place de Gaulle was bare of traffic save for a few cars parked forlornly at the curb, and some solitary figure sitting outside the large corner café.

Pierre drove down a narrow road to a tree-lined square and came to a stop in front of the Relais de la Poste, a subdued-looking restaurant whose interior – with its red-checked table-cloths and red-shaded lamps – was far more inviting than its outer façade.

They were served promptly by the *patronne*, who seemed to know Pierre well, and dinner, though not of the three-star variety, was an excellent example of Provençal cuisine, with an abundance of garlic and a profusion of delicious vegetables.

Replete, both as to food and wine, Miranda was no longer fearful as they drove down the wide, tree-lined Avenue Victor Hugo to the sea front. They went past several large blocks of flats and up a steep road bordered on one side by the sea and on the other by villas set back in their own grounds and reached only by long flights of steps. They continued to drive for several miles, climbing higher and losing sight of the sea completely until they reached a small square with a fountain set into a wall, and a signpost pointing to the Eden Roc Hotel. Here Pierre turned left, driving slowly down a quiet road unlit except for their own headlamps.

"This is the most exclusive part of the Cap," he explained. "Every house is owned by a millionaire."

They skirted a high brick wall and she knew instinctively that this marked the boundary of the Maurice estate. Sure enough, as a pair of gates came into sight Pierre stopped and flashed his lights three times. At once the gates swung open with an electronic whine for them to drive through.

"A millionaire's ansaphone service," he quipped, and Miranda looked through the rear window to see the gates close behind them.

A moment later they stopped at a wrought-iron door. It opened as if on cue, and a white-coated manservant ushered them into an octagonal marble hall, and then into an immense room overlooking the bay. One wall was of glass, and through it could be glimpsed softly lit lawns with clipped trees and shrubs, and beyond it the glittering jet sea and the silver-star-red sky.

The furniture was ultra-modern, with giant-sized armchairs in jewel-coloured suedes, interspersed with low tables in perspex and steel, and white fur rugs gleaming like snow on the black ebony floor.

A small, dapper man rose from an armchair to greet them. Silver grey hair and a baby pink complexion gave him a cherubic appearance at variance with the small eyes which flicked over Miranda like a scorpion's tongue.

"You are younger than I expected," he said.

"Today it's an asset to be young," Pierre put in easily.

Again the grey eyes surveyed Miranda. "I like your designs. They are original and they have a strong line. You could well be the person we are looking for."

"There's no doubt of it," Pierre intervened. "Miranda has an excellent reputation in England."

"I know. I have already found out." Monsieur Maurice beckoned them to sit down. "I assume you are prepared to work in Paris, Miss Dixon?"

"Of course."

"Good." The man picked up a folder and took out some of Miranda's sketches. "Are these what you envisage for next spring?"

"More or less."

"Don't forget Miranda designed her collection with no specific fabrics in mind," Pierre said quickly. "If she comes to Christi's she'll obviously work with *your* materials."

"Only if I like them," Miranda added, deciding there was no point in not being truthful. "I realise you finance Christi's, Monsieur Maurice, but I couldn't use fabrics unless I liked them."

The man sat as if lost in thought, then he stood up and pressed a button on the wall behind him. An entire section glided away and two rails rolled forward, weighed down with samples of fabric.

Never had Miranda seen such a host of colours nor so many different textures, from cobweb mohair to shaggy tweed, from heavy satin to finest chiffon.

"There you are," he said. "What do you think?"

"They're fabulous!" She fingered a supple jersey that glowed silver one moment and iridescent pearl the next.

"I designed more than half of these myself," Monsieur Maurice said. "I want you to know I am also a creator. My ambition is not only to make money, you understand, but to have beautiful clothes that will show *my* work to its best advantage."

Miranda warmed to the man for the first time since they had met. Here was an ambition she could appreciate.

"I think we would work well together, Monsieur Maurice."

"So do I."

"What are your terms?" Pierre said.

"The same I gave to José."

"He was a failure."

"When he came to me his reputation was greater than Miss Dixon's."

"Unfortunately *Christi's* reputation is lower now! Two bad seasons have harmed it – one more will kill it completely. You need Miranda far more than you needed José."

"What exactly are you asking for?" asked Monsieur Maurice.

"A bigger profit participation. Miranda would accept fifteen per cent in the first year, escalating to thirty in four years."

"That is out of the question – unless Miss Dixon can put up some money."

"Why do you need money?" Pierre asked. "Your company is one of the richest in Europe."

"Would a thousand pounds help?" Miranda inquired. "That's all I have."

"Wait!" There was excitement in Pierre's voice. "It might

be possible for Miranda to offer something much more important than money – something that would bring money into the company."

"Such as?"

"A perfume," Pierre said. "A perfume that would do for Christi's what Number 5 did for Chanel."

"You have such a perfume?"

"Yes."

Monsieur Maurice sat down and looked at them both.

Not knowing what Pierre was talking about, Miranda glanced at him covertly. He seemed oblivious of her look and lounged easily back on the settee as though he did not have a care in the world.

"May I ask what it's called?" Monsieur Maurice inquired.

"I'd rather not say until we have come to a satisfactory financial arrangement for Miss Dixon. Then you may evaluate the value of the scent for yourself."

"That will not be easy to do."

"Throw a cocktail party for a couple of hundred socialites and journalists and spray 'em!" Pierre said laconically. "I guarantee they'll go wild over it. Not only will the scent give you publicity, it'll bring in a fortune!"

"You are very confident."

"Because I know the scent, and because I'm prepared to do the publicity for it. Christi's needs *me* as well as Miranda."

Monsieur Maurice pursed his lips. "So it is the two of you I must engage?"

"Miranda is the most important one," Pierre said swiftly, "but I believe I can increase her value to you."

"You may well be right. If I can be convinced that the perfume is as good as you say, I will give Miss Dixon the percentage she wants. How soon can you let me have some of the scent?"

"Within a few days."

"Good. There is no time to lose. Our winter collection will

107

be shown in August, and that does not give Miss Dixon much time."

"I couldn't prepare a collection for *this* winter," Miranda said flatly. "Next spring is the earliest."

"Unless you could design our *next* collection I may have to reconsider my decision."

"I'm sorry." She was firm. "I don't intend to let myself be launched unless I'm ready for it."

Monsieur Maurice frowned. "You are obstinate."

"An artist has to be!"

Unexpectedly he smiled. "I like your honesty, so I will accept what you say. But at least prepare a few new designs for us."

She nodded, but before she could speak Pierre stood up to leave. His impatience surprised her, but she hid it. It was difficult to fathom what was going on in his mind. The perfume was but one example of this.

They walked to the door and were halfway towards it when it opened and a man and woman came in. Miranda stopped. Alain Maury and Colette Dinard were the last couple she had expected to see here.

"You are back early, Colette," Monsieur Maurice exclaimed.

"Alain promised Mother he would make up a fourth at Bridge." Colette kissed Monsieur Maurice on the cheek. "Why aren't you playing?"

"I've had business to attend to. I'd like you to meet –"

"I already know Pierre and Miss Dixon," the girl said.

Monsieur Maurice looked at Miranda. "I did not realise you knew my stepdaughter."

"We met a few days ago," Miranda said, and glanced at Pierre, annoyed that he had not told her of the relationship. Had she known, nothing would have induced her to consider a business partnership with the man. Even now it was not too late to turn it down; it would be embarrassing to do so, but less difficult than having to meet Colette frequently – and possibly Alain Maury too, if he married the girl! No, the very thought was impossible.

Blindly she caught at Pierre's arm. "We must go, we're keeping Monsieur Maurice from Bridge."

Not until they were bowling along the winding Cap road did she give vent to her anger.

"Why didn't you tell me he was Colette's stepfather?"

"What difference does it make?"

She bit her lip, knowing she was caught out. "I don't like her," she hedged, "and I don't want to be involved with her."

"You won't be. She doesn't take any interest in Monsieur Maurice's business – or Christi's."

"I still don't like it." Miranda tilted her head. "I don't want to be partners with her stepfather. I mean it, Pierre."

He slammed his foot so hard on the brake that Miranda was only saved from the windscreen by her safety belt. "You can't mean to let your dislike of Colette stop you from accepting the best offer you've had in your life!" She did not answer, and he swung her round to face him. "We're not talking about your refusing a dinner party invitation!" he stormed. "We're talking about your future. What does it matter who the hell Colette is?"

Put so bluntly, her reason sounded ludicrous. "I dislike anyone connected with Alain Maury," she said lamely.

"*That* part I can understand!" Pierre replied. "But I can't understand you throwing your future away because of some childish dislike of another woman. You're going to work at Christi's, dear cousin, whether you like it or not!"

He set the car in motion again, and she sat quietly, trying to analyse exactly why the French girl irritated her. It was not simply because she had been unfriendly from their first meeting: rather it stemmed from the fact that she was a close friend of Alain's. Anxious to concentrate on something else – indeed on anything that would push the man from her mind – she shifted round and looked at Pierre again.

"What perfume were you talking about to Monsieur Maurice?"

"None in particular. It was the first thing that came into my head."

She gasped. "He'll be furious when he finds out you invented the whole thing."

"I didn't exactly invent it. We *will* have a perfume. The blue rose."

"You must be joking!"

"It began that way," he confessed, "but as I kept talking it started to make sense. If you could launch a perfume like that, you'd be made!"

"I'm sure I would. But how do you suggest we get it? At knife-point?"

"We'll probably have to use a bit of persuasion," he conceded.

"Oh, be serious," she said crossly.

"I am. I've worked out a plan. Alain will do *anything* to grow those roses of his. Not only because it's the first perfume he's created in four years, but because the essence itself will make him a fortune."

"That's why he'll never give it to *us*."

"You don't understand. You can make more than one scent from an essence. The perfume he's got now won't be the *only* one he'll make from the blue rose."

Miranda looked searchingly at the profile beside her, and aware of her gaze, Pierre turned and smiled at her.

"It's true, dear cousin."

She relaxed. "I hadn't realised that. Mind you, I still don't think he'll sell it to us."

"He'll have to — if he wants the land."

"That's blackmail!"

"I prefer to use the word bargain!"

"We can't refuse to sell him the land," she protested.

"Why not? Tante Emilie's leaving the decision to me."

Pierre frowned. "Stop thinking in terms of one perfume. The blue rose is like sugar. Once you've got it you can use it to make a hundred different kinds of cakes. All we want is to buy Alain's first recipe. He'll make a handsome profit producing the perfume for us, but we'll get the profit from the sale and – more important still – all the publicity that goes with it. There'll be nothing to stop Alain launching any other perfumes at the same time."

Put like this, the proposition seemed workable, yet she was still doubtful if Alain Maury would agree to it. Even using Pierre's metaphor it could be argued that a cook might be more attached to the first recipe he had created than to any subsequent ones; possibly sufficiently attached to refuse to let anyone else have it.

"Creating a perfume isn't as easy," she said, remembering Madame Maury's comments on the subject as well as the bitter anguish which Alain himself had disclosed when referring to the barrenness of the years since Lucille's death. "What happens if he lets us launch the blue rose and then can't create anything else?"

"He will," Pierre said confidently. "He's one of the best in his field."

"He hasn't done anything for four years."

"You know the reason for that." Pierre looked at her again. "The fact that he's produced a perfume now shows he's got rid of his guilty conscience. It's probably because of Colette. There's nothing like one woman for helping you to forget another!"

The words brought with them a picture of Alain and Colette as she had seen them tonight. There had been an ease between them which spoke of familiarity, and it gave credence to Pierre's statement. Miranda was surprised at the bitterness this evoked in her. No matter how much she disliked Alain for his behaviour to Lucille, surely she didn't want him to go on

111

paying for it for ever? This was contrary to everything she had been brought up to believe. She sighed deeply, perplexed at the angry emotions which were tossing her around in a sea of confusion, washing away all her normal points of reference.

"Don't look so worried," Pierre said. "Think of the wonderful future ahead of you and leave me to deal with Alain."

"What will you say to him?"

"That he can buy the land on condition. . . . You know the rest. I don't need to say any more."

"No," she whispered, and wondered what Alain Maury would say when *he* was told.

CHAPTER EIGHT

Not expecting to sleep well, Miranda was surprised that her night was a dreamless one, and she awoke refreshed and elated. But her first sight of the landscape outside her bedroom window brought Alain to mind, and with it came the thought of his reaction to Pierre's proposal.

The idea was sufficiently daunting to destroy her appetite, and she sat on the terrace sipping coffee and wondering what the future held for her. How would her father react when he heard her news? It was one thing to suggest she come to Provence for a holiday, and quite another to discover that the holiday had led to her becoming a permanent resident of France and the chief designer at Christi's!

Her coffee cup clattered to the saucer. She was mad to have accepted such a position. How could she go from Mr. Joseph's wholesale house to a couturier one? Supervising two dozen girls in a workroom could not be compared with controlling a staff of several hundred.

Fear sent her to the telephone to call her father, and hearing his voice on the line, she precipitately blurted out her news.

"It's a big decision for you to take," he said finally. "I'll come out and see you. Then we can talk it over properly."

"I'd love that." She had not realised how much until she heard her father's offer. "When can you come?"

"In a couple of days. I've been wanting an excuse to see Provence again. It's time I laid *my* ghosts too."

His words stopped Miranda from thinking of her own problems. The last time her father had walked these sunny lanes he had met her mother, a meeting which had led to a few years happiness and far more years of loneliness. If his ghost *could* be laid, perhaps he might find happiness again.

"Come quickly," she whispered. "I'll tell Grandmother that—"

"I'll book in at the local hotel," he interrupted. "It will be better that way."

After the call, Miranda felt some of her confidence return, and she sat down at the library desk and began to sketch some new designs, raking her memory to utilise a few of the magnificent fabrics she had seen last night. The silvery jersey had made the strongest impression on her, and this gave creation to a host of evening dresses, all diaphanous and suggesting warm, sensuous nights. So intent was she on her work that Pierre's entry sent her pencil stabbing across the page, the point breaking in a spatter of carbon as she saw Alain Maury behind him. Why hadn't Pierre warned her that he was going to bring the man here?

Colour rushed into her cheeks, ebbing quickly as Pierre said: "Alain's agreed to manufacture the blue rose essence for us."

She had not anticipated such swift capitulation, and meeting Alain's mocking eyes, knew he was aware of her thoughts.

"Pierre is not the only realist, Miss Dixon," he said. "He knows how important it is for me to buy your grandmother's land."

"So it's all settled," she murmured.

"Yes," Pierre intervened. "Luckily Alain has several thousand cuttings ready in his greenhouses and they'll be planted out at once. It's a good thing we saw Maurice when we did. If we'd left the negotiations another week it would have been too late to plant the roses. As it is, the first blooms should be ready by September."

Surprise drew Miranda's gaze to Alain's. "Are they so late flowering?"

"They flower continually," he said. "That is another of their unusual features."

"It couldn't be more fortuitous." Pierre hugged Miranda

114

close. "I told you you wouldn't regret leaving everything to me."

Aware of the slim dark man behind her, she wriggled free. Not knowing how to change the conversation, yet knowing that she must, she pointed to her sketches. "I've been working too. I tried to remember some of the materials I saw last night."

Pierre looked at the drawings, and watching his face she knew he would make an implacable enemy. It was a good thing he was on her side. Yet it meant that Alain Maury was not. She was sure that his agreement to give her the blue rose had been an enforced one, and she glanced round and saw him watching her, his mouth so tightly set that the shape – which she had noticed and admired – had disappeared into a thin line.

"Take a look at these," Pierre said, handing him the sketches. "Then you'll realise why it's so important for Miranda to get every opportunity to succeed."

"I'm no judge of women's clothes."

Alain Maury held himself stiffly away from the designs, but Pierre thrust the sheets at him, forcing him to take them. Nerves or temper made him careless, and the sheets fell to the floor. Hurriedly he bent to pick them up, slowing down as he studied them.

Pierre caught Miranda's eye and winked. With the sunlight streaming in through the window to catch the auburn in his hair, he looked the epitome of a red devil, and she knew he had enjoyed forcing Alain to bend to his will. Again she wondered why the two men disliked each other so much. Pierre considered Alain guilty for Lucille's death, but surely this had not caused the break in their relationship?

With a start she heard Alain talking to her. "I can see why Pierre believes in your future," he said. "You have great flair."

"I'm glad you like them. I'll design a special bottle for the perfume too."

"Our own company usually does that," he said coldly.

"I'd still like to try. I know what appeals to women, and if the perfume is going to be launched as mine . . ."

The moment she spoke she regretted the words, for Alain flung her a look of such bitterness that she almost cried out.

"*You* can make the final decision, of course," she said breathlessly. "I'm sure you have more knowledge than me."

"What about a name?" Pierre said. "I've written out a list of suggestions."

"I'd like something simple," Miranda looked at Alain. "What do you have in mind?"

"Does it matter? The perfume's yours . . ."

She turned away, refusing to be swayed by pity. He had got the land which he desperately wanted, and to give her just one of the perfumes he would be able to produce from these lovely flowers was a small price to pay for it.

"I rather like the name Tendresse," she said slowly. "It's what most women want from a man."

"Most women don't deserve it," Alain retorted.

"Then at least let them be able to buy it!"

His laugh was sarcastic, and turning on his heel, he walked to the door, stopping as Pierre called after him.

"I'll get our lawyers to draw up a contract, Alain. I'm sure you'd like things settled."

"I don't go back on my word," came the reply, "and I don't expect you to do so either."

The door closed behind him and Pierre gave an angry snort. "He went back on his word four years ago and Lucille died because of it!"

"Oh, stop talking about the past," Miranda burst out. "It's all so morbid!"

"Sorry, my dear. I won't mention it again." Pierre smiled. "The future is much nicer, I agree – especially yours."

"And yours. You've acted as the catalyst in the whole situation, and I think we should be partners."

"No, no! It's *your* talent that got you the offer from Maurice, and your talent that will help you to keep it."

"But I want *you* to get something out of it too."

"I have the job I want. Publicity and advertising director for Christi's."

"What's so good about that?"

"I'll see you every day!" His grin disappeared. "You know what I'm trying to say, don't you?"

She shrugged helplessly. The conversation had taken an unexpected turn and she was dismayed by it. It seemed ungrateful to refuse Pierre's love, yet it was equally impossible to pretend she reciprocated it.

"At the moment I can't think of anything except my work," she hedged.

"There's no other man, is there?"

"No."

"Then I'll wait and take my chance."

"You can't mean that," she said uncertainly.

His head tilted quizzically. "I don't think you know *what* I mean, Miranda."

She thought about this at length when, alone in the library that afternoon, she put the final touches to her sketches. For all his warm personality, Pierre had a disregard for other people that showed itself in little, yet revealing ways. His casual teasing of Simone, who made her admiration of him so obvious; his ability to disarm the Comtesse and pretend the chateau meant so much to him – when she knew it meant so little; and his changing moods towards Miranda herself – cousinly one moment, loverlike the next, but always with an eye to the main chance. Pierre would make a typical French husband, she decided: attentive, loving and unfaithful. Not the partner for me, she knew with certainty, and firmly pushed away more dangerous thoughts about another man.

Pierre did not return for dinner that evening, telephoning from Nice to say he was still in conference with the lawyers who were drawing up the contract to send to Monsieur Maurice.

"I hope your French is good enough for you to read it," he concluded. "I can't have you signing something you don't understand."

"I'm prepared to rely on you – in business."

He chuckled. "I like your sharpness, Miranda. You'd never bore me."

She was still smiling at the remark when she returned to the table, but hardly had she sat down when the telephone rang again.

"Let Simone take it," the Comtesse admonished. "We are having dinner, not a running buffet!"

"It might be Monsieur Maurice," Miranda said. "I'd better go."

But the voice on the other end of the line was her father's, announcing his arrival at the Hotel de la Poste in the village.

"I never expected you so soon," she said happily.

"I felt you needed me."

"I do." She found it hard to keep the tears from her voice. "Let me tell Grandmother you're here."

"All right. But make it clear I came to see *you*."

"Can I come down to the hotel tonight, or are you too tired?"

"Certainly not. I'll meet you at the gates of the chateau. I don't like you walking around in the dark."

She returned to the dining room, where the Comtesse's sharp eyes immediately noticed her elated expression. "Don't tell me it was Monsieur Maurice who brought the pink to those cheeks?"

"Of course not."

"Alain, then?"

The pink became red. "What a thing to say!"

"A normal remark. He is a handsome young man. Or hadn't you noticed?"

118

Aware that her fork was trembling, Miranda dug it into a piece of veal. "It was my father on the phone. He's flown over to see me and he's staying in the village."

This time it was the Comtesse's fork that trembled, and seeing it, Miranda hurried to her grandmother's side. "Don't be upset, darling, he won't come here unless you want to see him."

"Naturally I will see him." The Comtesse's voice was quavery. "He should be staying here – not in the village."

"He didn't feel you'd want him to be here."

"He is your father and you love him. His place is in the chateau."

"I don't think so. It might be too much of a strain for you."

"It is a strain I should have faced a long time ago." Blue-veined lids momentarily lowered over the faded eyes. "I think I will go to my room."

"Aren't you feeling well?" Miranda asked nervously.

"A little upset. It is a shock for me to know your father is in the village again after so many years. The last time he was there, Louise was alive." She stood up, straight but frail. "Please call Simone to help me to my room."

"I'll take you."

"No, I insist you finish your dinner. I will be better once I am in bed."

Having promised to remain in the dining room, Miranda did so. It was strange to dine alone at the long, highly-polished table, carefully set with a few pieces of beautiful silverware and delicate lace mats. So must her grandmother have sat alone night after night, accompanied only by anguished memories of the daughter she had lost. How wasted the years had been, she thought sombrely, and vowed never to let bitterness warp her own judgment the way it had done her grandmother's.

It was with immeasurable relief that she finally hurried down the drive to fling herself into her father's embrace. She had forgotten how big and shaggy-looking he was, with his thick grey hair and calm smile.

Only as they sat in the lounge of the little hotel did she find a calm to match his, and told him of the sequence of events which had led to her meeting with Monsieur Maurice.

"The only thing that worries me is having to live in Paris," she concluded. "I don't suppose you'd give up the flat and join me?"

"Once you're settled, you won't want your old father hanging round you!"

"What rot! Anyway, you're not old."

"I must say I don't feel it." He waved his unlit pipe around the room. "Coming back here makes me feel thirty again. It seems only yesterday that I met your mother. I was going into the *boulangerie* to buy a *galette* and she was coming out with a loaf of bread. I bumped into her and knocked it to the floor."

Miranda hid her surprise. Only rarely had her father talked of her mother, and then there had always been sadness in his voice. But tonight he spoke prosaically, as if the trauma of coming here had finally laid his ghosts.

"Sometimes things are not as bad as you anticipate," he said, verbalising her thoughts. "The moment I saw the village again I knew I'd been a fool not to have come back before."

"Grand'mère feels the same," Miranda said. "She would like to see you."

"I'll call on her in the morning." He indicated the coffee pot and Miranda poured him another cup. "It's strange the way things have worked out for you," he went on. "I'm glad this Maury chap has agreed to let you market the perfume. It means you're in a stronger position with Maurice."

"That's what Pierre says."

"You don't seem very pleased by all that's happened."

"I will be, later on," she said. "At the moment I'm rather overwhelmed by it all."

"You need time to absorb it."

"Time's one thing I won't have. Pierre wants me to go to Paris to meet the staff at Christi's."

Her father gave a broad smile. "It will be a far cry from Mr. Joseph's!"

Miranda laughed. "I'd love to see his face when he hears! I'll give him a permanent seat at all my collections."

"So you think you'll last for more than one?"

"Dad!" Miranda exploded, and then giggled. "I never knew you had such faith in me!"

"Faith enough to tease you into laughing at yourself. That's one of your best qualities, my dear. As long as you can do that, you'll be able to deal with everything and everybody."

Not everyone, she thought silently; one man — silent and aloof in an ivory tower of his own making — would always elude her.

CHAPTER NINE

MIRANDA found very little to laugh about in the next few days. There was a detailed document of contract between herself and Monsieur Maurice to be read and absorbed; there was her father's meeting with her grandmother — an hour of tension which not even Roger Dixon's quiet humour had been able to lessen appreciably — and a frigid hour at the Maury laboratories in Grasse where she and Pierre had been shown the phial of scent which Alain had made from the first perfumed bush of blue roses grown on the Chambray land earlier that year.

"How much will you have ready for Miranda's first collection?" Pierre asked Alain, as they left the laboratory and made for the exit.

"If we have a good summer and autumn the supplies should be adequate by January. But if the weather is poor, it would be better to wait until next spring."

"I promised Monsieur Maurice we'd launch the perfume to coincide with Miranda's debut," Pierre said. "That means January."

"Will it make such a difference if you delay the perfume?"

"I've already told you. Without it, Miranda goes into Christi's as a highly paid employee with a bonus dangled in front of her like a carrot! But if she brings Tendresse with her, she gets a partnership."

"I fail to see why a six months' delay with the perfume should affect the situation," Alain said slowly.

"It does so from the publicity angle."

"We will do the best we can. But it really depends on the weather."

"If we're limited on quantity by January," Pierre answered,

"we'll still launch it – at double the price. If we make it the most expensive perfume in the world every woman will want it!'"

"Are you the arbiter of what women want?"

"Knowing the female mind has been part of my success!" Pierre smiled slyly at Miranda. "Don't you agree with me, *chérie*?"

"You don't need anyone to agree with you," she replied. "You are your own best audience!"

"On which happy note I will go and fetch the car."

He moved off, leaving Miranda alone with Alain. Neither of them spoke, and she shifted uneasily, aware of the lean, grey-suited figure beside her.

"Is the entire laboratory used for making perfume?" she asked, for want of anything to say.

"Yes. The cosmetics are made at our factory in Paris."

"It's strange that most cosmetic firms were started by women, yet fashion is predominantly created by men." She hesitated and then added, "Did you always want to work in this particular field?"

"I was originally a research chemist. I became interested in perfume by accident. I suppose you could say my nose led me to it."

She smiled, but there was no response on his face, which remained grave and withdrawn. Guilt tugged at her, but she forced it away. Alain Maury would concoct many other perfumes from the blue rose essence; it would make little difference to him to wait six months before bringing out another new one, whereas for her it would make all the difference in the world.

"I'm glad you let us have Tendresse," she murmured.

"I nearly refused."

"That wouldn't have been very businesslike."

"How do you arrive at that conclusion?"

"It's logical. I mean, you're just selling me the first cake –

"you'll be able to make many others to sell under the Adrienne label."

"What do cakes have to do with it?" he asked in glacial tones. "Or is this some type of English humour?"

"It was Pierre's metaphor," she confessed, and hurried through an explanation. "It wasn't until he told me that you'd be able to make several different perfumes from the blue rose that I agreed to let him ask you to sell us Tendresse."

"Wouldn't you have done so otherwise?"

"Of course not." She made her voice as firm as she could. "You haven't produced anything since your – since ... That made the blue rose very important to you."

"If you're referring to the fact that I haven't produced a perfume since Lucille died, then for heaven's sake say so! I'm well aware that – like everyone else – you believe me guilty of her death!"

"I d-don't know w-what to believe," she stammered.

"You astonish me. I thought my guilt was obvious." He flung out his hands. "You mean you don't think I *pushed* Lucille over the mountain ledge?"

"Don't be ridiculous!" Miranda gasped. "Of course you didn't!"

"But if she died because of me – because of what I did – I might just as well have pushed her. It's only a technical difference."

"Please," she cried, "don't say any more."

"Why not? Don't tell me you're tender-hearted about my feelings. If I'm not guilty of *actual* murder, I'm considered to have done it in a more subtle way. Surely the back numbers of *Nice Matin* didn't leave you with any doubts as to my innocence!"

Knowing it was useless to remain silent she forced herself to look directly at him. "I went to read about the case because I wished to know the *facts* and not the *prejudice* of other people."

"And what did the facts tell you?"

Unwilling to say, she was nonetheless unable to lie. Not that there was need for words; her difficulty in meeting his eyes told him what he wanted to know, and when he spoke again his voice was as icy as the waters into which Lucille had fallen.

"I am not concerned with what people think of me. I am only interested in living the kind of life *I* wish."

"If that's true, why are you so bitter? You don't like being thought guilty, Monsieur Maury."

"Even murderers like to pretend they're innocent!" he said cynically.

"How can you joke about a thing like this?"

"To joke is the only way one can live with tragedy."

"Was it a tragedy for you?"

Before he could answer, light footsteps approached and they turned to see Madame Maury coming towards them, graceful and serene in a cream silk dress and jacket.

"I didn't expect you here this morning, Maman," the man greeted her.

The woman smiled and put her hand on his arm before looking in Miranda's direction, her brown eyes dark with hostility. "I did not know *you* would be here, Miss Dixon."

"I've been given a tour of the laboratory," Miranda said quickly. "It was my first visit to a perfume factory."

"I suppose you came to see Tendresse?" The voice which Miranda had remembered as lilting was now frigid. "My son has informed me that he is giving it to you."

"We are buying it," Miranda corrected.

Madame Maury shrugged as though the money involved was unimportant. "Tendresse will be yours and not Alain's. That is all that matters. If –"

"Enough, Maman!" Alain Maury cut into the conversation. "I don't want any more discussion on the subject."

"Why shouldn't Miss Dixon know that –"

"Maman!" he said harshly, and Adrienne Maury lapsed into silence.

With immeasurable relief Miranda saw the red sports car approaching and murmuring goodbye, she ran down the steps and climbed in, looking back only to wave perfunctorily as she and Pierre drove out of the courtyard.

"That was a quick getaway," Pierre commented. "Was Alain being his usual charming self?"

"It was Madame Maury," Miranda admitted. "She's far more upset about giving us Trendresse than he is."

"You know how mercenary Frenchwomen are," Pierre shrugged. "She knows she'd make double the money if they launched it themselves." He squeezed Miranda's hand. "You needn't feel guilty about it, dear coz. I agreed to let Alain buy the land at a lower price, so financially they'll be no worse off."

"Oh, Pierre, I'm so glad you did that."

Seeing her pleasure, he smiled. "You're too tender-hearted. It's a good thing you've got me to watch over your interests."

Only later, as she sat in the library looking through the large swatch of patterns which had been delivered to her from Monsieur Maurice's factory, did she recall her conversation with Alain, and her mood of pleasure dissolved. He might not have pushed Lucille to her death, but his refusal to marry her had been tantamount to the same thing. As he had admitted!

He had known the girl was expecting his child; had known that her education and character had not given her the capability to cope alone with such a situation. Yet despite this he had refused to go through with their marriage, and because of it, he would never be able to disclaim guilt for her death. Yet how positively he had stated his unconcern about what people thought of him, even though in the same breath he had admitted that Lucille's death was a tragedy for him. But why was it a tragedy when he did not love her? Or was the tragedy caused by finding himself judged guilty of her death? To an ambitious man, this could indeed be tragic.

She thought of his beautiful house and the huge laboratories in Grasse. Guilt might have temporarily robbed him of his creativity, but it had not stopped him from continuing as a successful businessman. And now the success would be even bigger: the blue rose would see to that. Alan Maury's future was clearly defined: a road strewn with blue petals down which he would walk with Colette Dinard.

"Bother!" she said aloud, and flung the swatch of materials on the desk.

"Having trouble with your sketches?" her father enquired, coming in through the french windows.

"A bit."

"Perhaps you're concentrating too hard. Come out for a walk instead."

"Can I take a rain-check on that? I really must get on with some more designs."

"As you wish." Her father glanced at his watch. "I'm going back to the hotel. Can I get you anything?"

"Some biscuits. The ones shaped like crescents with nuts on them."

He nodded. "Will you collect them later and have dinner with me? I can recommend Madame Blond's cooking."

"I'd like that. A change of atmosphere will do me good."

Her father went out and Miranda concentrated on her sketch pad. She was still bent over it when a sudden glow of light made her look up to see Pierre in front of her, his hand on the desk lamp.

"It's bad to strain those beautiful eyes," he said.

"I hadn't realised it was dark."

"How's the work coming?"

"It isn't. I think I'm worrying too much about it."

"Are you surprised? You're bound to be nervous. But you'll worry less once you've seen Christi's for yourself. I've arranged for us to go to Paris tomorrow," he went on casually. "I hope that's all right with you?"

Her heart started to hammer against her ribs. "So soon?"

"The sooner the better!"

127

The prospect excited her, and only when she told her father during dinner did she realise ruefully that he might just as well have remained in London.

"Why don't you come to Paris with us?" she suggested.

"Can you see me amusing myself in a couturier's?" he chuckled. "That's your life, poppet, not mine. No, I'll be perfectly content to stay here till you return."

"I don't like leaving you."

"You left me alone in London," he teased. "Anyway, I've been invited out to lunch tomorrow by a very charming woman."

Uncertain whether she was being teased, Miranda looked at him. "What's her name?"

"Madame Maury."

"You're joking! You don't even know her."

"I do now – thanks to your almond-covered crescents!"

"What do you mean?"

"We were both in the *boulangerie* at the same time and we both asked for the last half-kilo they had!"

"I suppose you let Madame Maury take them?"

"Actually we compromised." Roger Dixon fished into his pocket and drew out a prettily wrapped package. "We took half each."

Miranda laughed. "I'll really enjoy these now!"

"You sound as if you don't like her."

"But I do. Unfortunately I don't think *she* likes me. It's because of the perfume."

"I see." Roger Dixon rubbed the side of his nose. "Would you prefer me not to see her?"

"What difference will it make?" Miranda half smiled to herself. "I just wonder if she would have invited you to lunch if she'd known you were my father."

"As a matter of fact we didn't exchange names till we parted. And that was two hours after we met!"

It took a moment for the words to register. "What on earth

128

were you and Madame Maury doing for two hours?"

"Walking and talking. After we'd shared out the biscuits I asked her to direct me to the local museum, and she decided to take me there herself. Then we explored some Roman ruins."

"I can see why you don't want to come to Paris," she laughed. "And here I was, worrying about you being lonely!" She looked down at her fork and, aware that something was troubling her, her father leaned across the table.

"What has this perfume of yours got to do with Madame Maury not liking you any more?"

"She's angry because we're buying it. Pierre thinks it's a matter of money. If her own company marketed it themselves, they'd make a much bigger profit out of it. But Pierre took that into account when he fixed a price on the land."

"Then you've nothing to feel guilty about. Would you like me to mention the price of the land to Madame Maury if I get the chance?"

Miranda frowned. "I don't think so. I'm probably making more out of her dislike than she meant. It's just that she was so friendly the first time we met, and I liked her so much that . . ."

"She has a great deal of charm," Roger Dixon agreed, and deliberately changed the subject.

It was midnight before Miranda returned to the chateau and, leaving her father at the gate, walked alone down the drive. In the moonlight the house looked like a fairy-tale palace, and she felt herself to be an enchanted princess caught up in a spell from which there was no escape. But to what was she bound? To this lovely house with its centuries of history, or to the glittering, unknown future? Unbidden her thoughts turned to the dark-haired man who seemed to be constantly in her mind, a man who irritated and annoyed her and, above all, frightened her.

For she was frightened of him, she admitted. Frightened of what he had done to the unknown Lucille and what he was now doing to her. She put her hands to her temples, surprised to find them damp. She was crazy to let this Frenchman occupy her mind. There was nothing so special about him that should have made her single him out. Yet she did not even have to close her eyes to see his face in front of her; the thin, straight brows, the firm mouth, the glittering brown stare.

The chateau door loomed ahead and she sped up the steps and inserted her key in the lock. Quietly she let herself into the hall and closed the door. Breathing deeply, she leaned against it to catch her breath. A table lamp illuminated the hall and in its warm glow her fanciful thoughts evaporated, so that once again she was the determined Miranda Dixon who knew exactly where she was going and with whom.

Mounting the stairs, she firmly resolved to think only of herself and her career.

Christi's fulfilled Miranda's greatest expectations. Set in a graceful house a stone's throw from the imposing Georges V Hotel, its opulent interior epitomised elegance and wealth. No woman would dare set foot here if she had to worry about overstepping her budget, nor would buyers come unless they could set down their minimum eight hundred pounds entrance fee which would entitle them to one *toile* – a linen pattern – from one collection. And the next collection, Miranda thought incredulously, was going to be hers!

The trepidation she had felt during the flight from Nice to Paris had left her the moment she was introduced to the *vendeuses* lined up in the salon to greet her. It was as though her years of training and the startling success she had achieved since leaving college had suddenly come to her aid, giving her the confidence with which to face the supercilious, condescending, curious and occasionally compassionate eyes regarding her.

Only as she went through the workrooms did nervousness return. Here was the hub of her empire; from this great heart would flow the blood to supply the sinews and muscles of this establishment. But looking at the last collection which had been produced, she realised how anaemic the blood had become, and how desperately in need of a transfusion the House of Christi was.

"You can see why Monsieur Maurice chose *you*," Pierre whispered to her as the last of a horrendous display of dresses fluttered out of sight.

"Where's the designer now?" she asked.

"He returned to Madrid."

"To bullfighting, I hope!"

Pierre laughed. "He had a good reputation, you know. Perhaps he was overwhelmed by everyone here."

"That happens to many designers. Look what a failure St. Laurent was when he started at Dior. Yet once he was on his own there was no stopping him."

"Don't *you* let anyone here intimidate you," Pierre said quickly.

"They won't. The designs I did for Mr. Joseph would knock spots off the ones I've just seen."

"That's my girl," Pierre laughed, and caught her hand to his lips. The gesture, so French, surprised her, for as always he looked more English than Parisian. "Monsieur Maurice is meeting us here at noon. The contract is ready for signature."

"I never knew lawyers could work so quickly!"

"Maurice doesn't want you to change your mind." Pierre glanced round the salon. "They've never sold perfume here before, so we must decide how to display it. I thought of turning the ground floor into a *parfumerie*."

Miranda shook her head. Until this moment she had not given the subject any thought, but instinct told her that Pierre was wrong.

"I'm going to make Tendresse the theme of my first collection," she said. "I'll use chiffon and velvet and sheerest wools. Everything must have movement. Lots of movement." She pointed to the walls of the salon. "We'll drape chiffon into the letter 'T' and suspend it all around. Just the one letter – not the whole word – it will be *your* job to make women know it stands for Tendresse."

"It *could* work," he said cautiously. "It could indeed." His voice grew more enthusiastic. "I like it. I know just what you mean. I'd better give *myself* a contract before you decide you can do your own publicity!"

She caught his hand. "I owe you too much to do without you, Pierre."

"Making yourself indispensable," a cool voice asked, and they drew apart as Monsieur Maurice and his stepdaughter came in.

"Colette," Pierre said, bowing. "I hadn't expected to see you here too."

"Why not? Naturally I'm anxious to know what's going to happen to Christi's."

Masking the chill which the words brought her, Miranda said easily, "I'm taking over, Miss Dinard. I thought you knew?"

"Only some of the details." Hard eyes raked her. "You surely don't intend to run the entire House?"

"I most certainly do. There can only be one person in control."

"That's always been Madame Vernier," Colette replied, and looked at her stepfather. "Haven't you told Miss Dixon about her?"

"We were too concerned over the main issue to worry about details."

"I'd hardly call Madame Vernier a detail," Colette said drily, and looked at Miranda. "She's been *directrice* here since Jacques Christi started. She has the loyalty of the workroom and every *vendeuse* behind her. If *she* doesn't approve of you, Papa will be crazy to bring you in!"

"Then it's a good thing the contract hasn't been signed yet." Miranda looked at Monsieur Maurice, who stared blandly back at her, unperturbed by his stepdaughter's remarks.

"I suggest we introduce you to Madame Vernier at once," he said. "She wasn't here when you arrived because she came to the airport to meet me." He motioned to a model who had been listening with undisguised interest to the discussion and she hurried out.

Everyone waited in silence, and Miranda braced herself for a difficult meeting. If Madame Vernier had started here with Christi himself she would no doubt have a fierce loyalty to the House, which would make her a formidable opponent of anyone whose ability she doubted. "She won't doubt *mine*," Miranda thought proudly, and tossed back her amber-gold hair, the only sign she gave of nerves. "I'm better than the other two men they brought in. I've got to remember that no matter what happens."

A short, plump woman bustled into the salon, and one look at the shrewd eyes set in the carefully made-up face allayed all Miranda's fears. A martinet the woman might be, but there was no doubting her intelligence nor her integrity. Miranda held out her hand and felt it taken in a firm grasp.

"Monsieur Maurice told me you were young," the woman said in faultless English, "but not *how* young!"

"Old enough to know my capabilities," Miranda replied with a faint smile, "and young enough to admit my limitations!"

Madame Vernier's chest expanded like a pouter pigeon as she acknowledged the full meaning of this remark. "I am sorry I was not here when you arrived, Miss Dixon."

"Never mind. Perhaps – if it won't inconvenience you – you would show me around?"

"You have already seen everything."

"Only with *my* eyes. I would like to try and see them with yours."

Madame Vernier's eyebrows rose, then abruptly she turned. "Come. I will show you."

Miranda's first introduction to the salon and workrooms paled into insignificance beside the one she received from Madame Vernier, and for the next three hours she followed the woman from room to room, and person to person, from the newest apprentice to the most experienced seamstress and cutter.

Gradually the great establishment came to life before her, its past glories reawakened both by the people she met and by the glimpses she was given of the great fashions which Jacques Christi had inspired, and which had been photographed and placed in leather-bound volumes in the *directrice*'s office. Patiently the woman explained how the great man had worked, showing her the dummies he had used to drape his materials on, the table where he had done his cutting and the desk where he had prepared his sketches.

"Since Jacques' death," Madame Vernier said, "we have existed on his reputation. The two designers Monsieur Maurice brought in were not big enough to wear his mantle, and luckily not big enough to destroy what he had built. But after two bad seasons we are beginning to falter. Another poor collection and we are finished."

"What do you think of *my* work?" Miranda asked bluntly.

"It is good. But putting designs on paper is only half the battle. Seeing that they are interpreted the way you wish — that their final appearance is the way you want them to be — takes determination and strength. This House has its own way of doing things, and if you are not strong enough, it can destroy you."

"I can be strong," Miranda replied, "as long as Christi's is on my side."

"I think it will be," Madame Vernier said, and caught Miranda's hands. "We have a great deal of work ahead of us. Will you be ready to design our winter colllection? We show at the end of August."

"I couldn't be ready before January," Miranda said regretfully.

"I was afraid of that."

"Why don't we just have small show for the winter?" Miranda ventured. "We could introduce a few of my clothes perhaps, and update some of the Christi coats and suits. After all, they're as famous as the Chanel ones, and *they've* been going for years!"

"An excellent idea. Christi coats and suits are timeless, but Señor Santos refused to put them into his collection."

"He must have been crazy!" said Miranda.

"Obstinate and conceited," Madame Vernier added.

"I can be obstinate too!"

Madame Vernier smiled. "A person is only obstinate if one does not agree with their ideas, but in the main I think I will agree with yours!"

Feeling as though she had come unscathed through the biggest battle of her career, Miranda returned to the salon to find that Monsieur Maurice and Pierre had long since departed, though to her dismay Colette had not gone with them.

"My stepfather has taken Pierre to lunch, but I thought we'd be more relaxed if we went somewhere on our own," she explained.

Aware that Colette's decision had not been prompted by liking, Miranda waited for the knife to be unsheathed. She did not have to wait long.

"Do you still feel so confident, now you've met Madame Vernier?" asked Colette.

"Even more so. She will be of enormous help."

"You're very young to take on such responsibility." Behind the beautiful mask of make-up, the girl's face was sharp. "Aren't you scared by it?"

"No."

"Then your imagination must be limited!" Colette's scarlet-tipped nails grasped her bag more firmly. "How do you plan to launch Alain's perfume?"

"It's Christi's perfume now."

"It will always be Alain's." Halfway down the stairs Colette paused to look at Miranda. "He hates you for taking it away from him. He'll never forgive you for it."

Miranda was glad she was holding on to the banisters, for the impact of the words made her knees tremble. "I'm sure that isn't true. Everything was arranged on a businesslike basis."

"Extremely *good* business on your part," Colette retorted. "If your collection is the biggest flop in the world you'll still make a fortune out of Tendresse. It was brilliant of Pierre to think of it. There isn't a woman in the world who won't want that scent."

"Do you know it?" Miranda asked, determined not to comment on anything else Colette said.

"Naturally. Alain gave me a phial. Apart from his mother, I'm the only person who has used it." The hard eyes were mocking. "But now it will be yours – though it won't do you any good."

"You've just said it will be a best-seller."

"Oh, it will bring you money, but it won't bring you Alain – and that's what you really want, isn't it?"

Miranda continued to walk downstairs. "I don't know what you're talking about."

"Yes, you do," Colette said behind her. "You've wanted Alain from the moment you met him."

"I'm not interested in men who jilt their pregnant fiancées," Miranda retorted, and could have bitten out her tongue as she heard Colette's laugh.

"I'll have to tell Alain you said that. I'm sure he'll find it interesting."

Blindly Miranda hurried down to the hall, waiting unseeingly for Colette to catch up with her. "Do you mind if I don't lunch with you?" she said, without looking round. "I've been concentrating so much with Madame Vernier that I'd like to go for a walk by myself."

"Of course," the French girl's normally sharp voice was sweet as saccharine. "But don't forget to come back. My step-father will be waiting for you."

"I'll be back," Miranda said, and set off down the tree-lined road, wishing she need never return; need never see Maurice or Pierre or the House of Christi again; and more particularly, need never see Colette Dinard.

The couple of days Miranda had anticipated spending in Paris stretched to ten, and she was once more caught up in the feverish excitement that seemed to go hand in hand with the fashion industry, whether one was in the cheap end of the trade or the most expensive. As Gertrude Stein might have said, she thought wryly on the tenth morning – "A dress is a dress is a dress."

She stepped back from the dummy on which she had been draping a soft wool georgette, one of several dresses she had designed this past week for the mini-collection that Christi's would be showing in August. With Paris blossoming from late spring into early summer it seemed ludicrous to be thinking of winter clothes, yet such was the pressure of the industry that one had to work months ahead of each season.

"I like that," Madame Vernier said approvingly, coming into the workroom. "It has a strong line."

"It's wonderful material," Miranda replied, "it drapes it-self."

"Everything that you design is workable. That's the mark of a couturier. You must know where you're going. If you don't, no one will want to follow you."

Miranda smiled and crossed to the window. It was uncur-tained to let in as much light as possible, and though at the top of the building, it was still noisy with the sound of traffic. In the room itself some two dozen *midinettes* were at work, needles flashing in and out of fine materials, and an occasional whirr of a sewing machine punctuated by a burst of laughter or conversation. Not that there was much chattering in Madame Vernier's presence, for the *directrice* ruled the establishment with an iron hand that saw no need of a velvet glove.

It was not an attitude which would have succeeded in London, Miranda knew, but then no one took fashion as seriously as the French, and any girl lucky enough to be taken on at a couturier's – even in the most lowly capacity – repaid the owner by long hours of eye-straining and back-breaking work.

Madame Vernier came towards her with a look presaging a command, and Miranda braced herself as she wondered what else was required of her. Unexpectedly it was a wedding dress.

"It always attracts good press coverage," Madame Vernier explained. "And I think you should do one."

"Wedding dresses are so banal," sighed Miranda.

"Not to the bride! If you have an idea of the line you intend to follow for your spring collection, perhaps you could give a hint of it with the wedding dress."

"That's an excellent idea." Miranda marvelled at the Directrice's astuteness. "I'll work something out when I get back to Provence."

"When are you going?"

"As soon as I can. I had no intention of staying away so long."

"You should be living in Paris already," Madame Vernier commented. "You must start to take control here."

It was a truth Miranda could not deny, and though she regretted that her stay in Provence must end, she knew it must if she wished to continue her career. If only it did not have to be in this most difficult of all cities! Paris might be gaiety and charm on the surface, but underneath it was a hard metropolis, much harder than London, yet with none of that city's efficiency.

138

"You will need to find a flat," Madame Vernier said. "If you could give me some idea of what you want. . . ."

Miranda shrugged away an answer. Until her contract had been finalised she was reluctant to commit herself. Besides, she had no real idea what money she could expect. She would have to discuss it with Pierre. She sighed. She seemed to talk everything over with him. Not an evening passed that she did not dine with him, nor a problem arise which she did not discuss with him. The faint unease he had aroused in her when they had first met no longer disturbed her, and she wondered if she had become used to his worldly cynicism or found it less noticeable because she was again living in a commercial atmosphere where achievement of one's ambition was the acme of success?

Yet her turning to Pierre was due, in part, to Colette Dinard. It was as if her awareness of the girl's relationship with Alain had made her conscious of her own barren life. It was not something that had worried her before, and she wondered wryly if it was the so-called magic of Paris that made her feel unfulfilled unless she had an admiring man to dress for and to live for.

Not that she could ever live for Pierre, she decided later that morning, as she waited for him to take her out for lunch. He was intelligent and amusing, but not someone with whom she would want to spend the rest of her life. There was no man with whom she could envisage doing that. No man.

She did not realise she had said the last two words aloud until she heard them repeated by Pierre, and turning from the mirror where she had been putting on fresh make-up, saw him framed in the doorway.

"What 'no man' were you referring to?" he quizzed.

"No man in particular! I'm too busy." She covered one side of her hair with a floppy red beret the same colour as the red buttons on her navy suit.

"No woman is so busy that she can't enjoy a little flirtation,"

139

he replied. "Anyway, I don't want to flirt with you. I'd like something more serious."

"At a quarter to one on a Wednesday afternoon?"

"At any time." The smile left his face and he looked grave. "You're my sort of girl, Miranda. We would make a wonderful team. You can't tell me you haven't felt that, too?"

She hesitated and then decided to be blunt. "Of course I've felt it. We work marvellously together. Half the time you know what I mean before I've said it, and the other half, you've gone and done it before I've even thought of it! But that doesn't mean it's love. In fact I know it isn't."

"How can you be so sure?"

"Because when I'm away from my work I'm *not* your sort of girl."

"You can't divorce yourself from your career. It's the very essence of you."

The word "essence" conjured up a narrow tanned face and a hard sardonic glance, and she pushed the image fiercely from her mind. "Three months ago I might have agreed with you," she said, forcing herself to concentrate on Pierre, "but now I'm not sure. Living in the chateau and learning so much more about my mother has made me realise what love can mean between two people."

"Knowing a person is a part of loving them," he retorted, "and you've just said how well I know *you*."

"The business side of me," she reminded him. "You know nothing of the other side."

"Show it to me," he murmured, "or let me find it out for myself."

Before she could stop him he pulled her into his arms and kissed her. Her resistance was instinctive, but he took no notice and continued to hold her, his grip tightening so that she could not move. Realising the childishness of trying to fight her way free, she remained quiescent in his arms, but it was like being held by a stranger, so calm and dispassionate did she feel.

The sharp click of a door drew them apart, and Miranda's face burned as she saw Colette and Monsieur Maurice watching them with amusement.

"It would be silly to say we hope we're not intruding," the girl said sardonically, "because we obviously are!"

"Not at all." Pierre sauntered over to the mirror and casually wiped the lipstick from his mouth. "Miranda and I were just going out to lunch."

"Were you having the hors d'oeuvres in the office?" Colette asked.

"I was sampling the sweet!" he said, and coming back to Miranda's side put his arm across her shoulders, a gesture that had now become second nature with him.

"I suggest we lunch together," Monsieur Maurice interrupted, his brusque tones cooling the emotional tension. "There's a clause in the contract we still have to discuss." He looked at Miranda. "It's about compensation if either of us wish to end the partnership."

"Do you still doubt Miranda's talent?" Pierre asked.

"*I* believe in it," Monsieur Maurice replied, "but will the public? Only time will tell, and if we are proved wrong. . . ."

"I wouldn't want compensation if you asked me to leave," Miranda said quickly. "Anyway, if I were no good I'd go without being told."

The podgy face creased into a smile, though the eyes remained shrewd. "I believe you would, Miranda, but you know what lawyers are — they like everything set out in black and white."

"Add whatever clause you think necessary and I'll sign it," she said, and stared at Pierre, defying him to disagree.

Knowing himself beaten, he shrugged and opened the door.

They lunched at Maxim's, the magnificence of the food suiting the quiet elegance of the decor. Miranda was amused at the intense way Colette and the two men discussed what they were going to eat, though the food, when it came, was worthy

141

of the care taken over its choice: delicious puff pastry cases stuffed with truffles and chicken breast, followed by sole in champagne sauce.

"I'll never get any work done this afternoon," Miranda said as she finally pushed away her plate. "When I'm working I rarely have anything more than coffee."

"That is bad for your health," Monsieur Maurice said.

"Maybe. But it's extremely good for my brain! Right now I wouldn't be able to tell a dress from a sauceboat!"

"I hope you're not really so sleepy," Colette drawled. "We're going to Alain's office this afternoon."

Miranda was glad that the folds of the tablecloth hid her trembling hands, and she looked enquiringly at Monsieur Maurice.

"Alain has brought some phials of Tendresse from Grasse," he explained. "It seemed a good opportunity to finalise everything with him."

"You don't need *me* there."

"A couple of points may arise that require your attention. It is better if you come."

He picked up the bill, then set down what seemed to Miranda an astronomical sum before leading the way out of the restaurant to his waiting car and chauffeur.

Within minutes they were deposited outside the double-fronted salon of Adrienne Cosmetics, which occupied a large corner block on the Champs Elysées. The interior decor was in variegated pastels which echoed the floral packaging of all the products, while the furniture was predominantly silver gilt, as was the ornate lift which took them to the second floor. Here the colours were strictly functional, and from behind closed doors came the sound of typewriters and telephone bells.

Miranda had no time for more than a fleeting impression of bustle and efficiency before Alain Maury came out of his office to greet them. In a dark, tailored suit he looked older and more austere than she had remembered, so that it was

142

hard to associate him with the passionate man she had run into on the lawn outside the chateau or the bitter and angry one she had encountered in Nice.

"A chair," he was saying, and she hurriedly perched on a spindly-legged one and forced herself to listen while Monsieur Maurice drew out some closely typed papers and began to go through them, with Alain making occasional terse interjections and Pierre smoothing over the frequent differences of interpretation that ruffled the conversation.

All the while Miranda surreptitiously looked at Alain. Lines of fatigue had etched themselves on his face and beneath his tan his skin had a greyish tinge. He looked every one of his thirty years, yet as he rubbed the side of his forehead with a clenched fist – the way a child often did when tired – she was overcome by such tenderness that she ached to reach out and touch him. Appalled by her weakness, she pressed back into her chair. He had only sold them a perfume; he had no right to look as bereft as though he had sold them his child.

His child.... Memory of Lucille corroded her thoughts like acid, eating away the tenderness she felt him. Tenderness. The name he had given to the first perfume he had created since Lucille's death. How dared he use the word when he did not even know its meaning!

Unable to bear her thoughts, she jumped up and walked over to the window. But nothing could shut out her awareness of the lean figure behind the teak desk, nor the slim, tanned fingers taking out three phials of perfume from a small box.

"This is for you, Miranda." Pierre came towards her with a phial in his hand. Unwillingly she took it, staring at the bare half-ounce of amber gold liquid, the same colour as her hair.

"As there's only so little," she murmured, "I don't think I should keep it. Can't you use it, Pierre? Give it to someone at *Vogue*, perhaps?"

"It's yours," he reiterated. "You said you were going to base your first big collection on Tendresse, so you should at least know what it smells like!" He swung back to the centre of the room. "Miranda has a sensational idea for the design of the bottle."

"So have I," Alain cut in, and from the drawer of his desk took out a gold-topped container. It was tall and narrow, perfectly plain except for a ripple of glass moulded to the front and forming a flowing letter "T".

Pierre's mouth dropped open, and he shot Miranda an accusing look. "You told him!"

"I never said a word." Disbelievingly she moved over and picked up the bottle. "This is the same idea as mine," she said, and looked directly into Alain's face.

Dark brown eyes stared at her, but there was nothing to be seen in their depths.

"Great minds think alike," he said coolly.

"It is good that you and Miranda are on the same wavelength," Monsieur Maurice smiled.

The silence was momentary yet uncomfortable, and was interrupted by Colette. "I adore your perfume, Alain, but I *don't* like the bottle. It's not dramatic enough."

"I prefer subtlety," he replied. "Besides, Tendresse is not a dramatic word. It is romantic."

Colette turned to Pierre. "Do *you* like the name?"

He hesitated. "It's going to be the theme of Miranda's spring collection."

"Christi's have always catered for the sophisticated woman," Colette said sharply, and looked at her stepfather. "You agree with that, don't you?"

"At the moment Christi's has no image. If Miranda feels the mood is towards romanticism. . . ."

Colette gave an angry toss of her head and subsided into silence. Again Miranda wondered whether it would not be wiser to abandon the idea of working in Paris. What peace of mind would she have if she constantly met Colette and Alain? It would be better to return to London and start up on her own. At least in that way she would be her own mistress.

Was Colette Alain's mistress? she wondered, and hastily pushed away the thought, furious at where word association had led her.

In an effort to quell the turmoil inside her, she moved closer to Pierre. "If there's no more need for me to stay, I'd like to go back to Christi's."

"It's far too late for you to work. I'll take you back to your hotel and we can have a quiet dinner."

"You should find a flat," Monsieur Maurice advised. "Madame Vernier spoke about it this morning."

Miranda could not help smiling. "She said the same to me."

"And me!" said Pierre. "But I've done something about it! There's a flat going in my apartment house. Three large rooms with a magnificent view over Paris."

Colette gave a sudden meaningful laugh. "It must be wonderful to meet a long-lost cousin and find he's not only handsome, but also so capable at managing your life."

"I wish I'd met him years ago," Miranda replied with commendable calm.

"You'd have been in your pram," Pierre said tenderly, and lifted her hand to his lips.

She suffered his touch with the smile still on her face, but was aware of Alain Maury pushing back his chair and closing the drawer of his desk.

"*I* will drive you back to your hotel, Miranda," he said, startling her not only by the offer but by the use of her first name.

She opened her mouth to refuse, but the look of fury on Colette's face made her change her mind, and she nodded.

A few moments later she was sitting beside him in a large black Citroën, watching as he weaved skilfully between the crush of cars. Unlike his compatriots he drove with quiet efficiency. No crashing gears or expletives marked his progress, merely a quietness that grew deeper the more thick the traffic became, until finally he gave a long sigh and, turning the car into a side street, parked it adroitly in what seemed to Miranda to be a minimum amount of space.

"It's hopeless to drive in the rush hour," he said. "Nothing makes me more bad-tempered."

"You don't look it."

"The angrier I get the quieter I become."

"You must be very angry now!"

He shrugged and folded his arms across his chest. "How do you think you will like working in Paris?"

"It will be a challenge."

"Will you cope?"

"Or die in the attempt!"

"You're too young to talk of dying," he said harshly.

"I didn't mean it literally."

"Then don't say such a thing. People talk too lightly of death."

She knew without being told that he was thinking of Lucille, and the knowledge was like a sudden stab of pain. "If you don't like driving in the rush hour," she said quickly, "you shouldn't have offered to drive me back to the hotel."

"I wanted to talk to you alone."

Her heart began to pound, but she said nothing, and waited for him to continue.

"It's about your father," he began.

She swung round at that. "He isn't ill, is he? I tried to call him last night, but I couldn't get through. Is that why –?"

"No, no, it's nothing like that." Seeing her fright, Alain instinctively put out his hands. They touched her breasts and he drew back sharply. "I'm sorry," he apologised. "I – you – your father's perfectly all right. There's no need to get alarmed."

"Then what –?"

"It's about his friendship with my mother."

Miranda stared at him. "I don't know what you're talking about."

"I realise that." For the first time there was slight humour in Alain Maury's voice. "That's why I wanted to talk to you ... to explain what has happened." He leaned against the wheel and the light from a street lamp fell obliquely across his face, catching the gleam of dark hair and the tightly stretched skin over bone. "They met in the village, as you know."

"And shared half a kilo of biscuits!"

"They now want to share their life," he said. "They've fallen in love."

Miranda was too astonished to speak. For years she had hoped her father would make a new life for himself, but never had she anticipated it being with a woman like Adrienne Maury: not only a wealthy successful tycoon but Alain's mother. No, it was impossible.

"Why is it impossible?" Alain's question made her realise she had spoken her final thoughts aloud. "They are old enough to know their own minds, and I believe they are well suited. If you were to see them together I am sure you would agree. Don't be jealous of my mother, Miranda. She will be good for your father."

Unwilling to have him misunderstand her reaction, she said quickly: "I'm sure they'll be extremely happy together."

"Then why is it impossible?"

"I was thinking about us. Our dislike of each other."

"I do not dislike you," he said slowly.

"But you don't *like* me?"

He hesitated even more noticeably. "That is true."

Depression weighed her down like lead. "Well then," she murmured, "now you know why I said it was impossible."

"We will have to hide our feelings for our parents' sake."

"Don't you think they'll guess?"

"No. At the moment they're too concerned with each other. And once they're married we will make sure we visit them at different times."

Again depression made it hard for her to reply, but knowing

147

he was waiting for her to speak she forced out the words. "Are you always so capable of settling people's lives?"

"One should do one's best to further a good marriage!"

"Or run away from a bad one?"

His breath hissed between his teeth and he gripped her arm and shook her. "Don't talk about Lucille!"

"I w-wasn't," she stammered.

"But you were thinking about her. Every time you look at me you think of her!"

"Can you blame me?"

"She's dead," he grated. "Let her rest in peace!" With an uncontrollable movement he pulled her against his chest, his head blotting out the light as he pressed his mouth on to hers.

Miranda's entire body responded to his touch. It was incredible that Pierre's lips left her so cold when Alain's awakened her to such desire, and even as she tried to resist it, her heart played traitor to her head, and her arms crept around his neck to caress the crisp, dark hair. Through the thickness of her jacket she could feel the thudding of his heart, but he spoke no word, merely kept kissing her with a growing intensity that began to frighten her. There was anger beneath his passion, a fury that she was afraid would become uncontrollable, and she pushed against his chest and tried to twist free of him.

"No, you don't!" he muttered thickly, and one of his hands clutched at her hair, twisting several strands round his fingers so that she could not move her head.

She pulled back even harder, the sharp tug at her scalp bringing tears of pain to her eyes. "Must you hurt every woman you want?" she cried. "Isn't it enough that you destroyed Lucille?"

His hands dropped away from her as though she were on fire, and she slid across the seat until the door handle dug into her spine. Beyond the car the traffic droned ceaselessly, but inside it was an oasis of quiet save for the heavy breathing of the man who slumped against the wheel, his head bent over his

148

hands. The anger that had given her the strength to pull away from him dissolved as she looked at him. How guilty he must feel if Lucille's name could still hurt him so much after four years. Yet if justice were to prevail, his conscience should never let him rest.

"I wasn't responsible for Lucille's death," he said suddenly, without lifting his head. "I want you to know that."

These were the first words he had ever said in his defence, and she could not hide her surprise.

"Then why did she kill herself?"

"I can't tell you that."

"Can't or *won't*?" He said nothing, and anger rose sharply inside her, made stronger by the knowledge of how much she wanted him to defend himself. "You changed your mind about marrying her," she accused. "That's why she died!"

"I *couldn't* marry her."

"Why not?"

He straightened, his face taut with suffering. "People change their – their minds. Can't you leave it at that?"

"No, I can't! Lucille loved you – she was going to have your child! Or didn't that mean anything to you?"

"Don't!" he burst out. "I don't want to talk about it."

"Because you've no defence!"

He remained silent, and the hope which had stirred in her when he had started to speak died away, leaving behind a bitterness she could taste. "I never despised any man more than you," she said slowly. "My only regret is that we'll have to meet again."

"I'm sorry."

"Is that all you can say?"

He did not reply. Instead he switched on the ignition and edged the car slowly out into the mainstream of traffic.

No word was spoken between them for the rest of the journey, and in silence they drew up outside her hotel. As the car came to a stop, Pierre hurried from the entrance to greet them.

"You left your perfume in Alain's office," he said, opening the door for her. "So I brought it along for you."

"You shouldn't have bothered." She flashed him her warmest smile, aware of the silent man at the wheel. "But I'll take you up on that dinner after all."

"Wonderful!" he said gaily, and helped her on to the pavement.

At once the engine raced into life and with a curt goodnight Alain streaked away. Watching the tail-lights disappear Miranda felt darkness envelop her, and even as it did, the light of revelation illumined all her past actions and thoughts. No longer did she need to puzzle over her reactions to Alain's behaviour or her tormented feelings every time she saw him or heard his name mentioned. She loved him. Had loved him possibly from the first moment she had seen his angry brown eyes over a taxi door.

Several passers-by jostled against her, and Pierre caught her arm and led her into the hotel.

"You look as if you need a drink." He steered her into the comforting dark of the small bar that lay to one side of the lobby. Leaving her at a corner table, he returned with two glasses and a half-bottle of champagne.

With a determined effort she made her lips curve into a smile. "What are we celebrating?"

"Nothing. That's the best time to drink champagne!"

It was an apt remark, and as the bubbles effervesced beneath her nose, she waited for the lift of spirits that drink would inevitably bring. Better to live with false pleasure than no pleasure at all.

"Drink up," Pierre ordered, "you're already beginning to sparkle."

"I was only feeling tired," she lied. "I'm glad you followed me."

"So I gathered."

She glanced at him beneath her lashes, but the blandness o

his expression gave nothing away. Yet to pretend she did not understand him would make both of them look foolish and she decided to tell him part of the truth.

"I quarrelled with Alain," she explained.

"Why?"

"We – we talked about Lucille. He said he wasn't responsible for her death and I – I didn't believe him."

"I'm not surprised. He must be crazy to think he can fool you."

"I still can't believe he acted so callously," she burst out. "I know he can be overbearing and obstinate, but I don't – I can't believe he's *cruel*."

"He isn't cruel," Pierre said in deliberate tones. "He just isn't capable of feeling love the way other people do."

"But Lucille was expecting his child!"

"I'm sure he'd have taken care of her financially. He wasn't to know she'd do anything so – so –"

"Don't defend him!" Miranda exclaimed. "What he did was despicable."

"I'm not defending him," Pierre said gently. "I'm trying to show you the sort of man he is. Don't be carried away by his looks or behaviour. He may be passionate on the surface, but underneath he's ice."

Remembering the way Alain had held her in his arms, Miranda found it difficult to hold her glass steady, and with trembling hands she set it down.

Pierre gave her a sharp look. "Don't tell me *you*'ve fallen for him?"

"Don't be ridiculous!"

"Then why did you look so shattered when you got out of his car?"

"Because I –" She moistened her lips, clutching hold of her senses in an effort to retain her secret. "Because he – because Madame Maury is going to marry my father!"

Pierre choked on his drink.

"It's true," she went on, and anticipating his questions, quickly told him how it had happened.

"So Alain's going to be your stepbrother," he mused. "No wonder you were upset."

"I've recovered now," she said quickly. "Alain and I have agreed that once our parents are married we'll make sure we visit them at different times."

"You can always take *me* along as watchdog!"

"I'm not frightened of him." She stood up. "I'll go and change."

"I'll come upstairs with you."

"I *am* frightened of you," she smiled. "Wait for me here."

He smiled back. "Put on something exotic and we'll go dancing."

Only as she left the bar did the smile leave her face. How would she be able to get through the long evening ahead and, more important still, the long lonely days of the future?

She must concentrate on work. That alone would be her salvation. Yet even her work would bring Alain close, for the perfume he had created was going to be an important part of her life.

Tendresse. . . . Tenderness.

But *his* tenderness was something she would never know.

CHAPTER TEN

WALKING across the tarmac of the Côte d'Azur Airport at Nice, Miranda was surprised by the sense of homecoming it gave her. Incredible to think she had only seen this coastline a few months ago; it was etched so clearly in her mind that she felt it had always been a part of her life.

Her father was waiting to greet her in the terminal hall, his hug warm and enveloping as he led her out to a small white Renault.

"I didn't expect to be met," she said as they drove off towards Bayronne.

"It seemed a good opportunity of talking to you. I take it Alain's told you the news?"

"Yes."

"Were you upset? I know it must be a shock for you."

"I'm delighted," she said quickly. "Though I must say it seems odd to congratulate your father because he's getting married! It makes me seem *de trop*!"

"You'll never be that." He slowed down and covered her hands with his own. "Nothing that happens to me in the future can alter the past. My love for your mother is something I'll remember all my life. But I've a chance to begin again with Adrienne and I'd be foolish to turn my back on it. She's a wonderful person. I'm sure you'll agree once you get to know her."

"I like her already. It's only a pity she –" Miranda stopped, unwilling to say more, but she had already said too much, for her father turned his head expectantly.

"What's a pity?"

"That she's Alain Maury's mother," Miranda said slowly. "He and I – we don't get on too well."

"Why not? He seems an exceptionally nice man."

153

"It's probably the disharmony of opposites."

"Usually opposites attract!"

"Not in our case," Miranda said with a forced laugh, and wished with all her heart that what her father had said was true. Yet even if Alain had reciprocated her feelings, the ghost of Lucille would always have come between them.

"When are you getting married?" She determinedly concentrated on other things.

"In a couple of weeks."

"So soon?"

"There's no point waiting. We won't change our minds."

"Are you that sure?" she asked seriously.

"Adrienne and I knew how we felt within a few days of meeting. It sometimes happens like that. Perhaps one day you'll know what I mean."

Her father's words threatened to play havoc with her self-control and she stared fixedly at the countryside flashing past.

"Tell me about your visit to Paris," her father asked, and for the rest of the journey she kept up a brisk monologue, painting him a word picture of the House of Christi and the work involved in running it.

"It seems an enormous job," he said. "Do you think you're up to it? You're so young."

"Twenty-two isn't young these days."

"I suppose not. But I'm glad *I'm* giving up the rat-race."

"I can't imagine you retiring," she commented.

"Not *complete* retirement. But any future engineering projects will have to be either in England or France. Luckily Adrienne's reached the stage where she can leave the business any time she wishes."

"Would she like to?" Miranda asked. "Most of her rivals died with their boots on — or perhaps I should say their make-up on!"

"Not Adrienne," Roger Dixon said firmly. "She's happy to leave everything to Alain."

In the distance the red-tiled roofs of Bayronne could be seen nestling against the hillside, while the village clock-tower pointed a dark finger into the deep blue sky. She had only been away a short while, yet summer had come to Provence and there was a languor in the air that had not been here before. The sun was hotter and the shade of the trees cooler as they bowled along the straight, wide village street, past the fountain chattering aimlessly to itself and the gaggle of black-clad women gossiping as they waited for the local bus.

She was relieved when they took the road to the chateau, though the relief evaporated as she climbed out of the car and saw Adrienne Maury coming along the terrace to greet her.

Resolutely pushing aside her embarrassment, Miranda kissed the woman warmly on both cheeks. The gesture was returned with an aloofness which had not been present the first time they had met. Despite her easy-going manner, it seemed that Madame Maury still resented being thwarted in business. But on the surface all was serene as the three of them went into the salon where the Comtesse was reclining on her favourite settee.

As though their entry had been a signal, Simone came in with coffee, and Miranda served it and then deliberately went to sit beside her future stepmother.

"I hope you're not upset at my marrying your father?" Adrienne Maury enquired gently.

"I'm delighted. I'm all for marriage!"

"You should start to think of it for yourself. Success and money can never be a compensation for personal happiness."

"I never thought it could."

The sloping shoulders moved as though the woman was about to say more, but evidently she decided against it, for she changed the subject and talked of a new three-star restaurant she had been told about.

Not until her father and Madame Maury left the chateau did Miranda have time to wonder at the meaning behind the woman's remarks. It was clear that in forcing Alain to let them market Tendresse, she and Pierre had aroused her anger. It was an emotion that did not fit the picture which Roger Dixon had built up of her. A woman who was no longer ambitious – who felt she had achieved enough in life to be able to take thing easy – should not be so furious at having to forgo the extra profit which would have come to her company had they sold Tendresse themselves instead of selling it in bulk to Christi's.

The hum of a motor interrupted Miranda's thoughts and she looked towards the horizon.

"It's Alain's men," her grandmother explained. "They are churning up the land as they plant the roses. Half the hillside is already covered. I'm sure you'll have your scent by next January."

"I hope so. Tendresse means a great deal to me."

The Comtesse smiled. "It's hard for me to think of you as a famous couturier."

Miranda laughed. "Is that wishful thinking, or are you psychic?"

"If one wishes hard enough one can often make the wish come true."

Miranda bit back a sigh. No amount of wishing could make her own dreams come true: the nightmare of reality made this impossible.

"When do you return to Paris?" her grandmother asked.

"At the end of the month."

"I wish you were a little less ambitious. I would like to see great-grandchildren before I die."

"I haven't found a man yet, darling – and please don't talk about dying."

"Could you not consider Pierre?"

Miranda shook her head. It was one thing to let Alain Maury think she liked Pierre more than she did, but quite another to pretend with her grandmother.

"I'm married to my work," she said firmly. "And right now

156

I've a wedding dress to design."

"How can you think like a bride when you don't want to be one?"

"That's what being creative is all about!"

Miranda remembered this remark several days later when, with a pad full of designs she did not like, she finally abandoned the idea of doing a wedding dress at all. Her failure to produce anything that even approximated her normal distinctive line made her conclude that the knowledge that she could never marry the man she loved was subconsciously preventing her from designing a dress for other, luckier girls to wear.

She was still musing on this when Adrienne Maury telephoned to say she was giving a party to introduce her future husband to her friends, and hoped Miranda and the Comtesse would join her.

"I'll be delighted to come," Miranda said, "but I'm not sure about Grand'mère."

In this her doubts were proved right, for the Comtesse decided she could not cope with the excitement of seeing so many strange people.

Miranda would have liked to stay away too, but knowing her father would be hurt if she did so, she put on a brave face and one of her smartest outfits.

Even so, she was unprepared for the vast throng that milled round the long buffet tables and spilled over the lawns down to the rose garden. The majority of people were French, though a smattering of other tongues could be heard.

Adrienne Maury looked delightful in soft-hued pink and made no effort to hide the love in her eyes as she led her future husband from group to group. Watching the two of them, Miranda expected to feel a spark of jealousy, but none came; all she felt was a gladness that after so many years of loneliness her father had at last found happiness again.

"You are feeling a little left out, perhaps?" a quiet voice murmured in her ear, and without looking round she knew

Alain was behind her.

"A little," she admitted. "But I'm very happy for them both."

"Good. So am I."

Knowing she would have to look at Alain some time, she turned and faced him. Seeing him with eyes of love she saw much that she had not seen before: the hardness of the jaw and the unexpected softness of the lower lip; the sharpness of glittering brown eyes and the tiredness of the myriad lines fanning out from them; the crispness of black hair and the blue-white look of the translucent skin on the temples, where a tiny nerve pulsed erratically. What a strange mixture of toughness and vulnerability he was! No wonder she was so muddled about him, her heart telling her he was one thing and her mind saying he was another.

Before she could speak, Colette appeared beside them, looking unexpectedly feminine in chiffon. "Your mother's looking for you, *chéri*."

With a slight bow he moved away, and Miranda gathered her confidence together to face the onslaught of Colette's dislike.

"Shouldn't you be in Paris working?" Colette demanded.

"I am not starting full-time until August."

"I don't see why not. You're getting a big enough profit from Christi's!"

Miranda refused to be drawn, but Colette required no response. "Provence seems to have worked wonders for you and your father. I bet you never expected things to turn out like this, when you first came here."

"I didn't expect anything except a few weeks' holiday in the sun." Miranda determinedly accepted the sentence at its face value. It took two to make a quarrel and though Colette was an eager first party, she had no intention of being the second.

"I'm delighted that my father and Madame Maury met. It

158

makes me believe in fairy tales."

"Have you met *your* Prince Charming yet?"

"I don't see *myself* as a heroine. I'm the Good Fairy, and good fairies never get married!"

Colette gave a ripple of laughter which yet managed to sound unamused. "Thank heavens *I'm* not a good fairy! Life without a Prince Charming would be awfully dull." The gleaming, coiffed head tilted to one side. "Don't tell anyone — Alain doesn't wish it known for the moment — but we're going to be married too."

It was news Miranda had anticipated, but even so she was unprepared for the shock the words gave her. The noise around her receded and grew louder as the blood rushed to her head. What sort of happiness would Alain find with a hard-faced girl like Colette?

"You don't seem very pleased at my news," Colette said softly. "I hope I haven't shattered your hopes."

"My hopes?"

"About Alain. Women find him so attractive that *they* do the running."

"I could never love a man I didn't trust." Irritation robbed Miranda of discretion. "And I couldn't trust someone who had already jilted another girl. Doesn't his past worry you?"

"I'm only concerned about his future. And I'm not so old-fashioned that I automatically blame the man when a girl becomes pregnant. It takes two to tango, you know!"

With an exclamation Miranda turned away. By showing her anger she had shown her jealousy too, and she must be careful to say no more in case she showed her love.

The thought of making more light-hearted conversation and pretend to a gaiety she was finding increasingly difficult to simulate decided her to leave at once, and she slipped over to tell her father.

"Adrienne and I would like you to have dinner with us in Cannes," he told her. "We've booked a table for a few friends."

159

"I've got a headache," she lied. "I wouldn't be very good company."

Her father's grey eyes were searching, but she met them guilelessly as she kissed him goodbye and hurried away. Even if he did not believe her, he was unlikely to do anything about it.

But in this she was wrong, for an hour after she had settled herself in the library, a blank sheet of paper staring her in the face as she again tried to design a wedding dress, the door opened and he came in.

"So much for your headache," he said bluntly. "I knew you were lying."

"I thought it better to do that than to tell you I had work to do."

"That would have been a lie too. You're only *finding* work to do because you don't want to have dinner with us." He placed both hands on the desk and stared at her squarely. "We've never lied to each other, Miranda, and it would be a pity if we started now. If you're unhappy because I'm marrying Adrienne I'd rather you said so and gave me your reasons."

Instantly she jumped up and ran round the side of the desk to stand close to him. "I'm delighted that you're getting married. Honestly. I'm only sorry you didn't meet her years ago."

"Then why did you run away just now? I want the truth — no more excuses."

She knew him too well to prevaricate any longer. Besides, to do so would only make the atmosphere more strained; far better to appear casual about it.

"I've already told you. I don't get on well with Alain, and I — I suppose Adrienne doesn't like me because of it."

"You *suppose*?" her father flared. "Don't you *know*?"

"Know what?"

"Why she doesn't like you?"

"Of course I know!" Miranda was too cross to be careful. "It's the money they're losing over the perfume."

160

"It's got nothing at all to do with money! In fact it beats me why Alain bothered to buy the land at all," her father said bluntly. "If I'd been him, I'd have told you to go take a running jump!"

It was a long time since Miranda had seen her father so angry, and she could not understand his reactions.

"Alain's a business man," she said quietly. "That's why he agreed to the arrangements. He'll make *some* profit out of Tendresse – and a fortune out of all the other perfumes."

"That's exactly what he can't do!"

"What do you mean?" She peered into her father's face. "What are you trying to tell me?"

"That the blue rose essence can only produce *one* perfume."

Miranda's breath caught in her throat. "Are you sure?"

"Positive. I don't know the technical details, but apparently this essence is so distinctive that it overrides every other scent that's blended with it. You might be able to alter the bouquet a little, but never appreciably enough to make another perfume."

Slowly Miranda absorbed what she had just heard. At last she understood Adrienne Maury's behaviour, though it made Alain's totally inexplicable. If he knew the blue rose could only be used for Tendresse, why had he agreed to sell it to her? Certainly she wouldn't have done so in his position. Better not to grow the blue rose at all than to grow it for someone else.

"Why did he sell me Tendresse?" she asked.

"Beats me. Perhaps just *growing* the rose is important to him. After all, he's spent years perfecting it."

"That still doesn't explain why he let Pierre think he could produce other scents from it."

"*Did* he say that to Pierre?" came the blunt query.

Again Miranda was overcome by shock. What a fool she had been! Loyalty to Pierre fought with honesty, and honesty won.

As though guessing her thoughts, her father said: "Pierre knew you wouldn't take Tendresse if he told you the truth."

"He had no right to lie to me!" She clenched her hands.

"How did *you* find out?"

"Adrienne told me. I was upset when you left the party this afternoon and I tackled her about her attitude to you. She's not a mercenary person, and she had to have a more personal reason than a profit motive. She knows what the blue rose means to Alain, and she was hurt for him."

"I can see why." Miranda's breath came out on a quivering sigh. "I couldn't use Tendresse now."

"There's nothing to stop you."

Miranda looked at her father bleakly. "I mightn't like Alain, but I know what Tendresse means to him – especially if it's the only perfume the blue rose can produce. I'll tell Monsieur Maurice at once."

"What will he do?"

"Alter our contract. But it won't make any difference to my decision."

"Pierre will try and make you change your mind," her father said.

"I'll have a thing or two to say to him!" she said vehemently. "When I think of the lies he told me –"

"He had your interests at heart," her father placated.

She did not answer; uncertain how much of Pierre's behaviour stemmed from a desire for her success or from the urge to hurt Alain. And it must have hurt him to have given up all the rights in his beloved blue roses.

"Pierre's flying down from Paris tonight," she said aloud. "He's coming with Monsieur Maurice."

"So you'll be able to tell them both?"

"Yes."

"Are you quite sure you want to?"

"Yes."

Her father came over to her. "Adrienne will be delighted."

"I'm not doing it because of you and Adrienne. I'm doing it because it's the *right* thing to do – the only thing!"

"I brought you up well," Roger Dixon said lightly.

"Too well, perhaps!" She put her hand on his arm. "Tell Adrienne I'll come and see her tomorrow."

"Why not tonight?"

"I want to talk to Monsieur Maurice."

"And Alain – when will you tell *him*?"

"You can do that for me."

"Oh no, my dear. That's something you'll have to do yourself."

Reaching up, she kissed her father's cheek, then walked with him to the door and watched him leave.

If Monsieur Maurice was unwilling to accept her without Tendresse, she would return to England and continue with her original plans. Perhaps it might even be better if she did, for it would at least put the distance of the Channel between herself and Alain.

CHAPTER ELEVEN

MONSIEUR Maurice was unable to see Miranda until late that evening, explaining regretfully that he had made dinner arrangements which he could not cancel.

"Why don't you and Pierre join me?" he suggested.

"I'd rather see you *after* dinner," she replied.

"You make it sound ominous." He paused as though waiting for her to say something, and when she didn't, he continued: "Let us make it ten o'clock, then."

Agreeing to this, she replaced the receiver. As she did so, she heard Pierre's car, and hurried into the hall to greet him before her nerves could play her false.

"I've just been talking to Monsieur Maurice," she said breathlessly. "I'm seeing him this evening."

"Any reason?"

"I'm not going to market Tendresse."

"Is this some sort of joke?"

"The joke was on me," she retorted, "and *you* played it."

"You'd better explain," he commented, and led the way into the salon. "Now then," he said as he closed the door "what's it all about?"

"I learned today that only *one* scent can be made from the blue rose."

"So?"

"So you should have told me. Tendresse belongs to Alain — not us."

"He agreed to let us have it," Pierre responded.

"Under duress! He wants to grow the roses and that was the only way he could do so."

"Well, he's *doing* so! Where's the problem?"

"It's a moral one."

"Morals mean a lot to Alain, I suppose?" Pierre sneered. "Grow up, Miranda. Selling us Tendresse will put a fortune into his bank account."

The words seemed a logical explanation for Alain's acceptance of Pierre's blackmail, and Miranda's feelings wavered. Was she being quixotic in her decision? Yet, quixotic or not, she would never rest until she had done what she planned.

"I don't believe Alain cares about money to the extent you're suggesting."

"Money's the *only* thing he cares about!" Pierre retorted. "Money and the freedom to do as he wants. He doesn't think the way we do, Miranda. He's obsessed with himself and his own importance."

"Maybe. But I still won't change my mind."

"You must. Everything's settled with Maurice."

"On a false premise. I'll go back to the original offer he made me before he knew I had a perfume to launch. It was a fair one, Pierre."

"It doesn't compare with the one you have now. If you go back to the original offer you'll just be a dress designer working for Christi's."

"I *am* a dress designer," she reminded him. "And I've got two choices open to me. Either I go it alone – in a small way – or I let Monsieur Maurice launch me in a big way as part of Christi's. And I know what I have to do."

"If you do it," Pierre said tightly, "you can count me out. I was willing to work like hell to promote Christi's so long as I knew you had a decent stake in it, but I won't work my guts out for Maurice!"

He swung away from her, and with a little cry she ran over to him.

"Don't be angry, Pierre, try and see it from my point of view. Tendresse means so much to Alain. It's like his child."

"That's the last simile you should use," he burst out.

His words stabbed through her, bringing Alain's past vividly close, and she clasped her hands to still their shaking.

"Don't do anything tonight," Pierre pleaded. "Sleep on it, Miranda. In the morning you may feel differently."

"I won't. I've made up my mind. Will you come with me to see Monsieur Maurice?"

"No. If you tell him, you must do it alone. I don't agree with you, and I won't be behind you any more."

"Is that your last word?"

His eyes were hard and shining. "Is it *your* last word?"

"I must do what I believe to be right."

"So must I." He put his hands in his pockets and teetered slowly backwards and forwards. "A few weeks ago I had an offer to work in America. I think I'll accept it after all. It will be better than watching you throw your future away."

The thought of not having him close at hand increased her feeling of being an alien in a foreign land, and she put her hands out to him. "Why won't you see it my way?" she pleaded.

"I can. I see a great deal. That's why it will be best if I don't work with you. You've fallen for Alain, Miranda. Like most women, you like a scoundrel."

It was safer to say nothing, and she turned away.

"You're crazy," he went on behind her. "Do you think Alain will ever look at a girl like you? A man just has to see you to know you've got wedding bells in mind! And those are the last thing *he* wants to hear!"

"You couldn't be more wrong," she retorted. "He's going to marry Colette."

Pierre's anger changed to amazement. "Doesn't knowing about Colette make you realise how stupid you're being over Tendresse?"

"What Alain does with his personal life doesn't affect what I decide to do with my business one."

For a long moment he stared at her, one strange expression

166

after another flitting across his face.

"You're a fool," he said finally, his voice flat and bitter, "and Alain's a bigger one!"

"Why do you hate him so much? Is it because of Lucille?"

"I always disliked him!" came the retort. "Lucille was just the final reason."

Miranda remembered these words as she sat in the back of the local taxi speeding down to Antibes. She had a vivid picture of Pierre as an impecunious young man living with his widowed mother in a beautiful chateau that was slowly crumbling into decay, while close by another boy – several years his junior, but fatherless like himself – was facing a glittering future. Pierre's envy must indeed have been deep for it to have lasted from youth through to maturity. How much this dislike had been increased by Alain's behaviour towards Lucille, she did not know, nor was she ever likely to find out, for Pierre would no longer confide in her nor help her. She frowned. He never *had* confided in her. Thinking over their many conversations she realised how little she knew of him. What would have happened if she had agreed to marry him? Would he have broken their engagement today? Somehow she knew that he would; knew too that his proposal had been born of expediency rather than love. But she could not find it in her heart to condemn him; rather did she feel a deep sadness that her idea of what was right should be so different from his.

Anticipating a difficult meeting with Monsieur Maurice, she was agreeably surprised that though his reaction was one of regret that they could not market Tendresse, he nonetheless understood and appreciated her decision.

"You had no choice," he agreed. "Every perfume Alain blends is part of himself, and with Tendresse it is even more so."

If only Pierre could have seen it this way, she thought, and said aloud: "I realise our contract will have to be revised, and I'll understand if you decide not to go ahead with it at all."

"And lose you completely?" Podgy hands shot up in consternation. "Madame Vernier would walk out with you! She is so convinced of your talent she would even follow you to London! No, my dear, we will leave the contract the way it is."

"But without a perfume."

"Forget it," he interrupted. "By keeping the contract the way it is I am being clever – not generous. If Madame Vernier sings your praises so loudly, then you are the right person to wear Jacques Christi's mantle. And once you make that mantle your own, you won't stay with me unless you are happy with your contract."

"I wouldn't go back on my word," she protested. "Money isn't that important to me."

"I realise that, my dear. And tonight, you have made it unimportant to me. The arrangements remain as they are – perfume or no perfume."

Pleasure warmed her; pleasure at having Monsieur Maurice behave so unexpectedly, and pleasure at being able to tell Pierre how wrong he had been. With her position remaining the same he would have no need to go to America. Yet even as she thought this, she knew it was not to be. Certain things could be forgotten, but some things – once said – could never be erased, and her horror at his implacable hatred of Alain was one of them.

Not that she herself would ever be able to hear the name Lucille without feeling pain at what he had done, but this did not give one the right to extract one's own vengeance.

She held out her hand to Monsieur Maurice. "Suddenly I'm not afraid of the future."

"I never have been." A door clicked and the man's eyes moved to it, his face creasing in a smile. "Alain," he welcomed, and Miranda turned to see him and Colette by the doorway.

"Don't you ever stop working?" Colette said, coming over to her stepfather. "Your weekends here are supposed to be a relaxation."

"It is not working to talk to Miss Dixon." He turned to Alain. "You must be delighted about Tendresse?"

Alain's brows drews drew together in a frown. "I beg your pardon?"

"You are obviously not on the scent!" Monsieur Maurice chuckled at his own joke, and then seeing Miranda's consternation, realised his indiscretion. "*Hélas!*" he said. "I have, as the English say, put my shoe in it!"

"Foot," Colette corrected. "But what are you talking about, Papa?"

"About Tendresse, my dear." He began to explain, and Miranda edged towards the door, wishing she could disappear through it without having to say goodnight.

With an effort she fought against her embarrassment, and felt the swift racing of her pulses subside, so that she was able to hear what he was saying.

"Why have you done it, Miranda?" Alain was speaking to her, a look of disbelief on his face. "I agreed to let you market Tendresse."

"I can't – not now. The blue rose means a lot to you. We both know that." She backed away from him and looked at Monsieur Maurice. "I'll see you again in Paris."

He nodded jovially and glanced at Alain. "You will surely offer Miranda a lift home? She came down by taxi."

"Of course," Alain said jerkily, and went to the door.

"There's no need to spoil your evening," she protested.

"It isn't spoilt. I am returning home anyway."

Within a moment goodnights were said and Miranda found herself sitting beside Alain in his car. It was the first time she had been completly alone with him since the night in Paris when he had driven her back to her hotel, and she could not help remembering the way he had pulled her into his arms and kissed her. She glanced at him, but he appeared oblivious of her presence, his eyes fixed on the road, his hands gripping the wheel so tightly that the knuckles gleamed white.

She wished she need not make any further reference to the perfume, but her father's marriage to Adrienne – which would make her meetings with Alain if not frequent, at least occasional – decided her to try and clarify the position completely. In that way there would be no more room for misunderstanding.

"I had no idea you could only produce one perfume from the blue rose."

"Pierre knew," Alain said coldly, not looking at her.

"*I* didn't."

The car engine raced as though the accelerator had been pressed harder.

"I didn't know," she persisted, "until my father told me."

"It needn't have affected your decision."

"Don't be ridiculous. Tendresse is yours."

"You knew that when you agreed to take it!"

"I didn't know it was the *only* scent you'd be able to make. ... I know what the rose means to you. That's why I couldn't take it."

The engine raced again, but the man at her side said nothing. Finally she could bear the silence no longer, and she turned to look at him. "Aren't you even a bit pleased?"

"Why should I be pleased to get back something which is rightfully mine?"

"You should at least be grateful I'm –"

"Grateful!" He stopped the car so suddenly that her head banged against the windscreen, and the sharp pain of it broke the final control she was holding on her temper.

"Yes, grateful!" she stormed. "If it hadn't been for Chambray land you wouldn't have grown your beastly roses in the first place!"

"You'd have liked that, wouldn't you?"

"Yes! You don't deserve to create anything beautiful. You're too evil and vicious!"

"I thought you'd soon start on my qualities! It's your favourite subject." He was angry as she had never seen him angry before, his eyes glittering like jet in a face that was bloodless. "How dare you set yourself up in judgment over me?"

"Why shouldn't I? I know the sort of person you are!"

"You know nothing!" he raged. "All you know is how to destroy a person!"

"You're the one who destroys!" she cried, and thought of the mountain ledge and the long rocky fall down to the ice-cold waters of the *vallon*.

"Leave Lucille out of it," he said in a deep, grating voice. "If you ever mention her again I'll kill you!"

"What's a murder to a man like you?"

"How dare you say that!" He lunged forward and gripped her throat.

She tried to struggle free, but she was powerless against his hold, and his nails dug into her skin.

"Save your energy," he rasped. "I'm not letting you go. Ever since I met you, you've been in the way. You've stopped me from thinking – from doing what I had to do!" He pulled her sharply forward, the rest of his words muffled against her mouth.

With all her strength she fought to push him away, but he pulled her closer still, his lips bruising in their intensity, his teeth drawing blood. She tried to stop the desire mounting inside her; to combat the fierce urge to respond, but she was powerless against the touch of his hands, against the pressure of his chest and the hard throbbing in the sinewy thighs that lay upon her own.

This was not the sort of love she wanted, this momentary flaring of the senses that would die out as quickly as it had erupted. Yet it was all Alain was capable of giving, all he *wanted* to give. Not for him a lasting relationship that would grow stronger with the years, but a few meaningless caresses from meaningless women who could be forgotten the moment they were out of sight. Or Colette, who was as tough and cruel as himself.

The thought of Colette was like a barricade against her senses, preventing her final surrender, and she struggled in his hold, hearing the rasp of tearing silk as she fought her way out of his arms.

"Leave me alone!" she cried. "I hate you!"

"You want me!" he mocked. "I felt the way you trembled."

"With hatred!" she cried. "Go back to Colette. She's the only woman you deserve!"

"You've a cruel tongue, Miranda. It's your best weapon."

"Because I tell you what you are?"

"How do you know what I am?" His voice was bitter. "It's a good thing you're not a judge. You'd never bother with prison sentences. As far as you're concerned no one could expiate their guilt even if they spent a lifetime behind bars!"

"You're right," she panted. "I could never forgive a murderer!"

He drew away from her, the fury draining from his face. "A murderer," he echoed softly. "Yes, you have made me feel more like one than any woman I've ever known."

There was a desolation in the words that made her ache with pity for him. But she mustn't pity him. She must despise him; it was her only salvation.

"You feel what you *are*," she told him, "and I'm sorry for you."

Silently he switched on the ignition and concentrated on the ribbon of road unwinding in front of them. His profile was forbidding, his brows drawn together in a scowl. No need to ask if he ever sat in judgment on himself: the lines either side of his mouth were sure indication that he had, as were the years when he had struggled – and failed – to produce his perfume. Remembering the viciousness of her words she was appalled, but knew that to attempt an apology would be worse than useless. Some things, once said, could never be forgotten.

Only when they reached the chateau did he speak to her.

"Even for my mother's sake I can't face the prospect of seeing you again," he said. "We'll have to meet on the day of the wedding, but after that, make sure you keep away from the house when I'm at home."

"Don't worry," she retorted. "I don't want to see you either!"

"Not even to call me a murderer again?"

"Now *you're* talking about Lucille," she pointed out, jumping from the car.

"Only as an epilogue. Believe me, I felt far more like killing you than I ever did her!"

Before she could think of a suitable retort he shot down the drive as if all the demons of hell were after him.

As they deserved to be, she thought, and closed the door of the chateau, wishing she could just as easily close Alain from her mind.

CHAPTER TWELVE

IT was mid-morning before Miranda awoke. Her sleep had been heavy and dreamless, and she lay for a long while in the large bed, hearing the creak of the shutters and wishing that the hills outside were the hills of Hampstead and not Provence.

Memory of the night before washed over her and, like a sea of sand, scratched against her consciousness, so that she sat up irritably and reached for her dressing gown.

By the time she made her way downstairs it was well after eleven, and deciding not to bother with breakfast she went into the kitchen to make herself some orange juice. Simone greeted her with a dourness reminiscent of her earlier unfriendly attitude, and Miranda, wondering what had caused it, soon learned the reason.

"Monsieur Maurice has gone."

"To Grasse?"

"To Paris."

Miranda concentrated on the thick yellow juice she was pouring into her glass. "Did he leave a message for me?"

"He said nothing. He spoke to the Comtesse, though."

Glass in hand, Miranda went in search of her grandmother, whom she found on the terrace. As always the old lady had made no concession to the weather and a mohair stole covered her head and shoulders.

"I understand Pierre's gone back to Paris," Miranda said, kissing her good morning. "Did he say why?"

"He gave me a reason, but I do not believe it was the real one."

The words were an indication of the Comtesse's intelligence, and Miranda abandoned the idea of lying to any questions that might be asked.

"He said he had only come down to say goodbye to me before going to America," the Comtesse continued. "He is thinking of accepting a job there."

"He told me the same."

"Does that mean he won't be working with you at Christi's?" And at Miranda's nod: "What about you? Are you leaving France too?"

"Of course not. My plans are unchanged."

"Then why did Pierre's plans alter?"

"We had a quarrel. Pierre lied to me about Tendresse." Perched on the edge of a bamboo chair, Miranda recited a carefully monitored account of the events of the night before, omitting entirely her final scene in the car with Alain.

"You did the only thing possible," the Comtesse said at last, her voice a breath of sound no stronger than the faint breeze stirring the clematis that climbed the stone pillars of the terrace. "I am sure Alain can create another perfume for you to launch – if you wish him to do so. It won't have the exceptional properties of Tendresse, but at least you need have no guilt at selling it as your own."

"If Christi's launch a perfume," Miranda replied, "it won't be Alain's. My one aim in life is never to see him again!"

"The young are so positive in their assertions," the Comtesse sighed. "I suppose when blood runs hot, the feelings run high!"

"Alain makes my blood run cold," Miranda said crisply.

"Don't sit on judgment on anyone, my child."

The words were so similar to Alain's that Miranda jumped up, knocking over the glass of juice as she did so. "Now look what I've done!" she cried, and tears of exasperation rushed into her eyes, telling her more clearly than words how on edge she was.

The day stretched unendingly ahead of her, and had it not been for upsetting her grandmother, she would have returned to Paris immediately. Memory of all she had said to Alain kept reverberating in her brain, while her mind's eye pictured him with Colette. Was the French girl able to rouse him the way she herself had done? It was difficult to imagine Colette abandoning herself to love, though there was no doubting her possessive attitude. Poor Alain! She could almost pity him being married to such a woman.

Thought of Colette as a bride made Miranda realise she might be asked to design the wedding dress. Though the girl normally patronised other couture houses, Miranda was convinced that spite would bring her to Christi's. What torture it would be to make the dress that would also make her Alain's wife.

"Is anything wrong, child?" the Comtesse asked. "You didn't cut your hand on the glass, did you?"

Miranda stared at the empty tumbler in her hand, realising that her silence of the past few moments had been misunderstood.

"I'm fine," she said hastily. "I was just day-dreaming."

"Are you very upset at Pierre's departure? I know you were fond of him."

"I'm glad he's gone. He behaved badly, Grand'mère. There's no point pretending he didn't."

"He did it because he wants the best for you."

"He wanted the best for himself."

Even as she spoke, Miranda felt there was something she did not understand about Pierre. If he had been solely concerned for his own advancement he would have accepted her offer of financial participation in her arrangements with Monsieur Maurice. Yet he had point-blank refused to do so, expressing himself perfectly satisfied to act as publicity director for the company. But somehow she was convinced there *had* been an underlying reason behind his determination to get her the best deal possible, even though it had meant lying to her about Tendresse.

This brought her back to Alain. In his place she would rather have abandoned the entire rose project than let someone else market the single perfume it could produce.

With a sigh she took the empty glass back to the kitchen. She was thinking in circles; it would be as well to concentrate on something else. She glanced at Simone, who was standing by the stove stirring the contents of a large black pot from which came a delicious smell of hare and wine.

"Lovely," Miranda said, sniffing. "Is it one of your own recipes?"

The woman grunted. "It is Monsieur Pierre's favourite. I wouldn't have done it if I had known he was leaving."

"I'm sure my grandmother and I will enjoy it just as much." She set her glass down on the draining board. "Monsieur Pierre's going to America, Simone, so he may not be back for quite a while."

The woman said nothing, though her face had a pitifully mottled look that roused Miranda's compassion. "But I'm sure he'll come back for holidays and to see Grand'mère."

"I'm used to his being away," Simone said staunchly, the wooden spoon in her hand moving vigorously in the pot. "After Mademoiselle Lucille died he was afraid to come back for more than a year."

For a long while Miranda stared at the casserole, her own thoughts quietly simmering. "Why was he afraid to come back?" she asked finally.

"I don't know what you mean."

"You said he was afraid to come back for more than a year after Lucille died."

The thickset shoulders lifted. "I did not mean anything by it."

"You must have meant something," Miranda persisted. "Why did Monsieur Pierre stay away?"

"He was upset because of the tragedy," Simone said stonily. "We all were."

With a flash of inspiration Miranda felt she was glimpsing the truth. "Was Monsieur Pierre in love with Lucille?"

"What if he was? It's all over with now. The past is finished. Dead."

"I was only curious." Miranda made an effort to be casual. "As you say, it doesn't matter any more."

There was a flash in the dark eyes before the veined lids rolled over them. "Yes, he loved her. That's why he stayed away afterwards." The lid clanged back on the casserole and Simone moved over to the table and began to roll out some dough that had been resting in a bowl; her elbows moved as she kneaded and pummelled, and watching the continuing rhythm and the shuttered face, Miranda knew she would learn no more.

As always when she felt troubled, she went to the library. The sunlight streamed in through the windows, warming her shoulders, and she relaxed against it, feeling some of her tension ebb. It had been stupid of her not to have guessed that Pierre had loved Lucille. It explained his animosity towards Alain and why he had driven such a hard bargain over the land and the perfume.

She wondered why he had hidden his feelings for Lucille. Had he told her, it would have made her much more understanding of his behaviour. She glanced at the telephone. Perhaps she would call him in Paris. Yet if she did so, he might decide to come back – especially once he learned that Monsieur Maurice had left her contract untouched.

She shook her head and wandered aimlessly round the room. She did not want to work with Pierre. His hatred of Alain went too deep, would keep Alain vivid in her own mind too.

Stopping by a bookshelf, she picked out a hand-tooled leather book depicting eighteenth-century costume that she was using as a reference guide. Forcing her mind back to her work, she rummaged through the pages of the book. The delicate drawings were a joy to see, and she studied the details of the costumes carefully, making copious notes and redesigning some of the accessories and embroideries to be more evocative of the twentieth century. She was still absorbed in her task when the gong sounded for lunch, and she hurried to wash her hands before going to the dining room.

At the table she forced herself to make conversation, and though she did not have much appetite, the casserole of hare was so delicious that she ate a normal serving.

"You look flushed, Miranda," her grandmother commented.

"I've been concentrating," Miranda smiled. "You've some wonderful old books in the library, Grand'mère. Some of them must be valuable."

"A few of them were printed especially for the family."

"I had no idea."

The Comtesse smiled. "If you come across any marked 'Edition Dauphin' they were printed for us in Paris in 1810, when the Chambrays still had money."

"I think I'm working with one of those books now," Miranda said, and ran into the library to fetch it. "Yes, it is," she said, coming back with it in her hand. "How exciting to think it's one of our own."

"You'll find several more if you look. There were three different ones of that edition you're holding."

"I've only found one."

"The others are definitely there. Three years ago a couple of students stayed here for a holiday and repaid me by cataloguing the books. If any had been missing they'd have mentioned it. You have no idea what a state the library was in before they tidied it. Books everywhere. Pierre was always promising to put them away, but he never did, and Simone just dusted them and put them back in the same old piles. Now of course it's as tidy as a public library!"

"I'll look for those other two books later. If they're fashion ones I'd love to find them."

Returning to the library at the meal's end, Miranda started

to sketch again, but the lunch she had eaten coupled with the warmth of the room made her drowsy, and she closed the book and pushed back her chair. If she went on sitting here she would fall asleep. Determined not to get into the siesta habit, she decided to look for the other two books right away.

Methodically she began to scan the shelves. It became clear to her why the books were in such disorder; the students might well have catalogued them, but they had not put them back in any order. If she wanted to find the two she was looking for, it would require more than a casual glance along the shelves. Deciding to do it systematically, she carried over a small antique pair of library steps to the furthest corner of the room and began her search from there.

It was slow work, enlivened by the occasional discovery of an interesting book either beautifully bound or with unusual illustrations. Soon the rows of shelves opposite the window had been examined and left, and she concentrated on the ones facing the door. There were no signs of any books from the Dauphin Press, and she climbed the ladder to complete her search of the topmost shelf. One ponderous title after another passed before her eyes, but there were no books on fashion. She had better settle for the one she already had.

Even as she decided to end the search, her hand came to rest on dark brown calf, and with trembling fingers she drew out two books of equal size and shape to the one on her desk. With an exclamation of pleasure she flipped through the first few pages. Yet, thus she had come to the end of her search.

Clasping the books close, she descended the ladder. As she reached the last step her heel caught in the rung and she lurched forward. Afraid of hitting her head, she put out her hands to save herself. The books thudded to the floor and she fell on top of them, the breath knocked out of her body.

For a moment she remained on the carpet, then quickly scrambled to her feet. She bent and picked up the books, examining them carefully to make sure they were not damaged.

Apart from one page being crumpled, they seemed intact, and she gave a sigh of relief and closed them.

As she did so she noticed one of the pages sticking out at an angle. Hurriedly she opened the book again, stopping in surprise as she saw it wasn't a page jutting out but a separate sheet of paper in the same grey parchment colour. It was a handwritten page with delicate flowing writing. And not written in the nineteenth century either, but in the twentieth.

From four years ago, to be precise. . . . From Lucille.

Miranda's knees gave way and she sat down abruptly, surprised at the emotion engulfing her as she held the letter in her hands. The writing was large like that of a child, the script unmistakably French and a replica of the one she had seen in the yellowing pages of *Nice Matin*.

Without being aware of doing so, she read a few words, and only then realised that the letter was addressed to Pierre. But what was a letter from Lucille doing in this book? He had obviously received it and slipped it between the pages for safe keeping until he could either file it or throw it away. It was odd he should have left it here, though. Suddenly she smiled. He must have put the letter in the book and then gone off for the day, a habit she had noticed he had during his stay here. During his absence the students had obviously started tidying the library and had tidied away the letter at the same time.

Pleased by her logical deduction, Miranda looked at the letter again. The last L and E was blurred, as though the ink had been rubbed by water, and with a sudden stab of pity she realised the blob was a tear-mark.

She knew she should put the letter away unread, but curiosity was too strong to be denied, and despite a feeling of guilt, she started to read it.

Quickly she scanned the lines, and as their meaning became clear the page shook so hard in her hand that she had to rest it on the desk. More slowly, she read it a second time. The writing was scrawled and some of the sentences were unfinished, but despite this the plea came through with heart-rending clarity: a plea for a man's love and help – as she had expected – but Pierre's.

Pierre. . . .

It couldn't be true. Yet there was no denying it. It was here for her to see in black and white. Lucille and Pierre had been in love. Or at least he had pretended to be, for he had obviously changed his mind, and Lucille's letter begged him to tell her he did not mean it.

"You can't have stopped loving me," she had written. "Not after all you said – the things we did. . . . It's useless to pretend nothing has happened. Alain doesn't know the truth, but I'm sure he suspects, and I'm going to tell him he's right. A few weeks ago you might have convinced me I should keep silent, but I can't do so any longer. Adrienne has been like a mother to me and for her sake I must tell Alain the truth. I can't become his wife when I'm carrying your child! It's too much to ask of me."

Several words were too blurred to be deciphered, as though tears had fallen faster at this point, and Miranda skipped them and read on.

"I'll be at the usual place this afternoon, and I'll wait there till you come, no matter how late it is. You mustn't leave me, Pierre. If you do, I can't face this alone. Nor can I ever do as you suggest. If the child dies, I will die with it."

The name "Lucille" marked the end of the letter, as it marked the end of everything Miranda had believed about Alain.

The truth was so staggering that it made coherent thought difficult, and for a long while she sat without any clear awareness of the passing of time.

No wonder Pierre had left the chateau after Lucille's death and had not come back for more than a year! And how clever of him to accuse Alain and to foster the accusation so that it remained as strong in people's minds today as it had been four years ago.

Fury brought her to her feet. Why hadn't Alain defended himself? How could he have let the scandalmongers go on crucifying him? Slowly, inexorably, the answer came to her, as it would have come a long time ago if she had had any sense. Loving Lucille the way he had – and she was prepared to believe that now – he had guessed her feelings for Pierre, and after her death and the discovery that she had been pregnant, he had known that to assert his own innocence would mean besmirching her memory even more and, regardless of the consequences, he had remained silent.

In a large city the pregnancy and death of an unmarried girl – whether it was accident or suicide – would have aroused comment for a few days and then been forgotten. But in a village like Bayronne the story had lived and flourished, reaching out evil tentacles to stifle Alain's life for years, making it impossible for him to continue with the work he loved. It was not the stench of his own guilt – as she had so cruelly said – which had prevented him from creating other perfumes, but the bitter knowledge that he had been let down by the woman he loved and the man he had hero-worshipped as a boy. It was amazing how she was remembering all the things Alain had said to her on the subject and how – since the discovery of this letter – the cast such a different light on it. The light of truth.

Holding the letter in her hand, she went upstairs to her room and put on a pair of flat-heeled shoes. She had to give this letter to Alain and apologise for everything she had said to him. Nothing less would do. The thought of what he might say to her was daunting, but she refused to be put off by it.

Slipping a cardigan over her shoulders, she hurried out of the house. She was halfway down the drive when she chided herself for not having telephoned first to make sure he was at home. Yet to have called and told him she was coming might have caused comment and forced her into an explanation. No, it was better to go unheralded and talk to him face to face. The letter crackled in the pocket of her dress and she began to run.

She was breathless by the time she reached the village, but here luck was with her, for she recognised the young man coming out of the *boulangerie* as one of the servants from the villa.

Obligingly he let her ride on the back of his motor cycle, depositing her outside the front door in the time it would have taken her to walk twenty yards.

"Is Monsieur Maury at home?" she asked breathlessly as she climbed off the bike.

"Yes, *mademoiselle*."

Another thought struck Miranda. "And Miss Dinard?"

If Colette was here she would be unable to talk to Alain. It was impossible to make her apologies in front of that ice-cold woman. Yet ice-cold or not, Colette had shown greater loyalty to Alain than she had herself. The thought smarted, and she burned with the shame of it.

"Miss Dinard is not here," the man said. "Only the family. But if you want Monsieur Alain, you will find him in the conservatory. He is always there at this hour."

Miranda sped round the side of the house and found herself facing a glass door. Nervously she turned the handle and went in. Despite the warmth outside she was struck by the moist heat billowing around her. The heavy scent of exotic blooms hung in the air and her eyes ranged from one colourful plant to another. A huge cactus masked part of her view and she edged past it and down the narrow aisle. This was more like a glassed-in ballroom than a conservatory, she thought, and stared in bewilderment at a never-ending vista of greenery.

She came to an intersection and paused. The trickle of water sounded in her ears and she moved in the direction it came from, her steps faltering as she skirted some dangerous-looking spiky leaves and saw the slim, dark-haired man bent over a small pot. In it was a straggle of wispy leaves and an amber gold flower that reminded her of a columbine.

Unaware of anyone watching him, Alain was not monitoring

his expression, and it was half sad, half tender as he bent over the tiny plant, his fingers exploring the leaves as gently as they had explored her last night. Emotion flooded through her and she must have given a gasp, for he started and turned, his expression hardening as he saw her.

"What are *you* doing here?"

"I came to see you – to say how sorry I –"

"Forget it," he said harshly. "We both said more than we should have done last night."

"I shouldn't have said *any* of it!"

"There's no need to demean yourself," he said wearily. "Let's be civil about it and go back to our original plan of pretending to some form of friendship for our parents' sake."

"I can't," she blurted out, and stopped, digging her hands into the pockets of her dress. It was going to be hard enough to tell Alain the truth without completely losing face and letting him know she loved him. Paper crackled beneath her fingers and she took out the letter.

"Read it," she said in a ragged voice. "It's from Lucille."

"For God's sake!" he exclaimed. "I thought we weren't going to talk about her any more."

Ignoring his remark, she thrust the letter into his face, and with a slow, almost reluctant gesture he took it from her and began to read.

Watching him, Miranda saw the colour ebb from his face, leaving it as grey as a corpse. Unable to bear the sight of it, she turned away and stared at a group of plants, counting the leaves and then, when she had reached two hundred, counting them again.

"Where did you find this?" His voice was devoid of expression. He might have been asking her what time it was.

Equally coolly she gave him the answer, telling him also how she thought it had come to be in the book.

"You're probably right," he replied. "Pierre must have got the letter and then shot off to Cannes. I know he was there at

185

mid-morning and didn't leave till midnight . . . by which time Lucille was dead."

"How could he have run away like that?" Miranda whispered. "He knew what she'd do. She couldn't have put it more clearly."

"He wanted her to do it. It was the best way out for him."

Miranda shuddered. "*He's* the murderer! When I think of the things I said to you. . . . How can I apologise?"

"There's no need. You were not alone in thinking me guilty."

"Why did you *let* people think it?"

"I had a duty to Lucille."

"I knew you'd say that!" she exclaimed. "But what duty did you have to a girl who let you down the way she did?"

"Because I let *her* down." He averted his head so that she could only see his profile, with a lock of dark hair falling over his forehead and a muscle twitching in his cheek like a pulse. "I became engaged to Lucille without loving her. I did love her, of course, but as a member of the family – as my mother's goddaughter who had grown up with me – not the love a man should have for the woman he's going to marry."

"And Lucille knew this?"

"Yes. Her feelings for me were the same. Our marriage would have been one of convenience. A happy one, I am sure, but without the *grande passion*." He glanced at her momentarily. "It is hard for you to understand our French customs, I suppose, but such a marriage is not unusual even in this day and age."

"I know that," she said stiffly, "but I wouldn't have thought you'd have wanted that kind of marriage!"

"Wouldn't you?" Again he glanced at her. "Last night you seemed very sure I had no love to give anyone."

"I merely meant that I didn't see – still don't see you – as loving anything except your work."

"I didn't at that time. That's why marriage to Lucille

seemed a satisfactory solution. Neither of us would have made great demands on the other." He paused and looked down at the gold plant in front of him. "Then gradually I sensed a change in her. I was certain she had fallen in love with Pierre and I waited for her to tell me. When she didn't, *I* decided to tell *her*. It seemed foolish for us to pretend. Pierre was single, and if they loved each other. . . ."

"He didn't," Miranda whispered.

"I realised that when she denied the whole thing. She swore I was imagining it."

"When did you find out it was true?"

"On the morning of the day she died." Alain rubbed the side of his face wearily. "She had discovered she was pregnant and she told me the whole story and gave me back my ring. I was very bitter – as you can imagine – and we had a row. I went off to Grasse and left her. She wrote me a letter then – the letter that was found in her pocket after she killed herself. It was the letter you read in *Nice Matin*."

Remembering the interpretation she had put on it – that everyone had put on it – Miranda's cheeks burned with shame.

"Why did you take the blame for her death?" she whispered.

"Because if I'd really loved her she mightn't have turned to Pierre."

"That's nonsense. A moment ago you said your marriage would have been one of convenience."

"Lucille was an impressionable girl. If I'd spent more time with her – if I'd cared for her – she might have fallen in love with me."

"And perhaps she mightn't," Miranda said crisply, compassion giving way to anger that he should have allowed his good name to be usurped so quixotically. "It was crazy to think like that. Pierre behaved like a swine and you took the blame for it! Surely for your mother's sake you could –"

"My mother knew the truth."

Miranda was astounded. "And she let you go on with the

pretence?"

"She felt I should do what I wanted."

"*I* wouldn't have let you do it," Miranda said fiercely. "You were a fool!" Tears blurred her eyes and she rubbed them away with the back of her hand. "I'm not going to apologise to you after all! Why should I blame myself for believing the worst of you when you encouraged everyone to think so?"

"The people who knew me," he said softly, "knew I wasn't guilty."

"But you never told them?"

"No."

Miranda lowered her eyes. Implicit in his words was Colette's belief in his innocence, or perhaps Colette had not cared either way.

"It was kind of you to bring me the letter," he said suddenly. "It at least confirms that Pierre knew what she intended doing."

"That's the worst part of it all. I'm glad he isn't here now," she said savagely. "If he has the gall to come back to the chateau I'll throw him out!" She tilted her head. "I'm going to tell my grandmother the truth."

"Why bother? She is old, and the shock could be harmful."

"She's a Chambray," Miranda said fiercely, "and she wouldn't thank me if I kept her in ignorance. Pierre acted despicably, and the facts should be known."

"You must tell no one else. I've protected Lucille's name for four years and I intend to go on doing so."

"At least you love her now," Miranda said shakily.

"I know what love means," he corrected, "and because of that, I know what she missed."

She absorbed his words slowly, finding the message they bore to be a painful one. His marriage to Colette was obviously not one of convenience, but the *grande passion* he had never felt for Lucille.

"So you're in love at last?" she whispered.

"Does that surprise you?"

"Not really. I don't suppose you'd get married otherwise. Not that I like your choice." She bit her lip. "I'm sorry, I shouldn't have said that."

His brows rose. "What's wrong with my choice?"

"You know without my telling you."

"I'm afraid I don't. Please go on."

"I have no actual reason," she shrugged. "You could call it mutual antipathy. It's the way *we* felt about each other the moment we met."

"We did?"

"You know we did!" she said sharply. "And that's what I feel for Colette. So don't let her ask me to design her wedding dress, because I won't."

A strange light glittered in Alain's eyes. "Won't you do it even for me?"

"No."

"Not even if I begged you to do so?" He came a step closer. "Not even if I told you that unless my bride wore your dress I wouldn't marry her?"

"Don't!" she cried. "Don't be cruel!"

"Cruel?" he repeated, looking astonished.

"Yes," she said, and burst into tears. "You know I love you. You must know, or you wouldn't be so heartless."

"I'm certainly heartless," he groaned, and pulled her violently into his arms. "You took my heart the moment we met."

"No! You don't mean it!"

"Don't I?" he said against her mouth. "I loved you from the moment I saw you at the chateau."

"No," she said again. "Not after the way I behaved . . . the things I said. . . ." She pulled slightly back from his hold. "What about Colette? You're going to marry her – she said so!"

"Wishful thinking, I'm afraid. I have never proposed to her. Never!" he affirmed. "Not even when I was furious with you."

Tears blinded Miranda's eyes. "When I think of all the awful things I said to you. . . . I must have hurt you so much."

"You did. And I was sorely tempted to hurt you back."

"Then why did you agree to Pierre's blackmail over the perfume? You should have refused to buy the land — refused to grow the roses."

"I grew them for you. I knew of your arrangements with Maurice and what the perfume meant to you."

"I didn't deserve it." Her tears fell fast. "You make me feel so small . . . so mean."

"Don't talk like that about the woman I love!" He wiped her tears away with his hand. "You will take Tendresse back —"

"No! It's yours."

"It's *ours*. Your success will be mine."

"Oh, Alain!" Her tears flowed again. "I don't know what to say."

"Thank heaven for that," he said, and gently moved his lips against hers.

"Alain, I —"

"No more words," he whispered. "We've a lifetime ahead for explanations. Right now there's only one thing I want to do."

"What's that?" she asked, starry-eyed.

"I'll show you," he replied.

And did.

Accept FOUR BEST-SELLING ROMANCES FREE

You have nothing to lose—and a whole new world of romance to gain. Send this coupon today, and enjoy the novels that have already enthralled thousands of readers!